Dear Anthony, Hi there on Blue Power Ranger Ward. As you can see, we do have e-mail. It's great, isn't it? I love e-mailing all my friends but I'm not allowed to go on any chat lines in case of perverts and I can't stay on for ever because of the ££$$£££. We got it during the summer. Jem, my mum's partner, needs it to find acting work because he's resting at the moment.

It is the start of Year 8 at Bartock High and stuck-up Anthony Bent is in hospital having his appendix out. He has his lap-top computer with him and Simone offers to keep him up to date with all the news—and his homework.

But Simone has enough problems of her own to deal with. Her mum is pregna___ d Simone is worried that Jem will prefer the new baby. Perhaps s___ should go to live with her dad? And what will all her friends at ___ol say about her mum having a baby at her age? And on top of ___his, Simone has just started to learn German and has to help desi___ web-page for the school. How on earth can she cope with all ___ different things whirling round in her brain? Perhaps e-mailing ___ony will help her sort things out.

Helena Pic___aty (Pierre-li-hatty) was born in Sweden to an English mother and ___olish-Russian father. An ex-teacher, Helena now writes full-time and lives in Nottinghamshire with her husband and two children. *Simone's Website* is her eighth novel for Oxford University Press.

Other books by Helena Pielichaty

Simone's Letters
Simone's Diary
There's Only One Danny Ogle

After School Club:
Starring Sammie . . .
Starring Brody . . .

For older readers:
Vicious Circle
Getting Rid of Karenna
Jade's Story
Never Ever

Simone's Website

Helena Pielichaty
Illustrated by Sue Heap

OXFORD
UNIVERSITY PRESS

OXFORD

UNIVERSITY PRESS

Great Clarendon Street, Oxford OX2 6DP

Oxford University Press is a department of the University of Oxford.
It furthers the University's objective of excellence in research, scholarship,
and education by publishing worldwide in

Oxford New York

Auckland Bangkok Buenos Aires
Cape Town Chennai Dar es Salaam Delhi Hong Kong Istanbul
Karachi Kolkata Kuala Lumpur Madrid Melbourne Mexico City Mumbai
Nairobi São Paulo Shanghai Taipei Tokyo Toronto

Oxford is a registered trade mark of Oxford University Press
in the UK and in certain other countries

British Library Cataloguing in Publication Data available

ISBN 0 19 275289 8

1 3 5 7 9 10 8 6 4 2

Designed and typeset by Mike Brain Graphic Design Limited, Oxford

Printed in Great Britain by
Cox & Wyman Ltd, Reading, Berkshire

for Oscar

Acknowledgements

With thanks to Andrew Grant for his gallant attempt at
showing me how to design a web page, Carole Wall for
sharing her knowledge on children's reading habits, pupils
at Ansford Community School, Castle Cary and Haywood
School, Nottingham for their enthusiasm and poems.

Special thanks go to Gillian Cross for
'taking part' in Book Week at Simone's School.

Get Well Soon

STARS IN YOUR SIZE
Costume Hire for Wonderful Disguises in all Shapes and Sizes

High Street Bartock (above Wibberley News)

Tel: 01384 – 789010   Fax: 01384 – 789344

Dear Anthony,

Find enclosed a card from us all. Sorry if it seems a bit battered—the wobbly writing and crumpled corners were because I was trying to get Peter Bacon to sign it on the bus which was never going to be easy with his wrist just out of plaster and the way Hazel, our bus driver, takes the bends. The other bits are down to Pete's brother, Luther, who snatched it off him when he found out it was for you and messed it up even more. I thought about getting another card to start again but Dad only had ones with soppy flowers or kittens left in his shop so I've tried to Tippex out the stuff Luther wrote because it wasn't very savoury. Anyway, here's your card. You can always hide it behind the others on your bedside cabinet. Are you on Blue Power Ranger Ward or Red Power Ranger Ward? I'm usually on Red when I've been in hospital with my asthma but Blue always gets the magazine trolley first and has a better view of the river.

Hope you're feeling better after your appendix exploded.

Best wishes from

Simone A. Wibberley
on behalf of your 8DC classmates

Blue Power Ranger Ward
Bartock Royal Infirmary
Bartock

September 14th

Dear Simone,

First of all, please excuse the scribble but even a
week after the event I am still frail from my
emergency appendectomy and even the simple act of
putting pen to paper exhausts me. There may well be a
view of the river from here but I am far too fragile
to peer out of windows yet, alas. You are probably
unaware of just how serious my condition was, S, so I
will tell you. My appendix ruptured (not exploded—do
try to use the correct terminology) and this almost
led to something called peritonitis. I hate to be
morbid but it could well have been a rather different
card you were sending, if you know what I mean, had
it not been for the skilful surgeons at BRI.

   Actually, the card is the reason I am writing to
you, S, seeing as you were the only one who put
anything decent on the pitiful thing, even if it was an
apology written on poorly reproduced stationery.

   When I finally managed to prise the card open (do
allow the Tippex to dry first—it's a _basic_) I was
astounded and appalled by the lack of signatures. I
believe there are thirty-seven students in 8DC? I
counted only eight genuine names and seven bogus ones.
(Do tell Peter Bacon no one appreciates his puerile
sense of humour. I recognized his chronic handwriting
as both Eileen Dover and Ivor Bigbutt. Tell him to
grow up.)

So, my question is, has there been a flu epidemic at Bartock High while I have been drifting in and out of consciousness? It seems the only explanation. After all, I was captain of the Y7 Swimming and Orienteering teams last year, two highly successful and popular activities.

What irks is when I compare that card to the one Peter Bacon received during Activities Week at the end of July when he—let's face it—dived, on purpose, off the climbing wall the army had brought in. Result? One tiny broken wrist. For that self-inflicted injury he was inundated with novelty balloons, cards (note the plural), and an assortment of unsuitable confectionery guaranteed to keep him hyperactive until his late teens. As you live near them you must be more than aware of the mental instability of the Bacon family so I'm sure you can see why I feel peeved, S. In a nutshell, I am not impressed with my classmates' efforts so far. Perhaps you can organize some kind of collection for me—you're good at that sort of thing—but make sure you avoid displaying the results on public transport. An accompanying card with a kitten upon it would be perfectly acceptable. I have a cat called Magnus O'Puss who is the love of my life.

Yours, at the point of exhaustion,
Anthony Bent

PS: I don't suppose you're on e-mail by any chance? Mother has just brought me my trusty laptop, much to the amusement of the nurses for some reason. It would make life so much easier vis-à-vis homework etc. if I could have your address. Mine is: bent.ant@macro.com.

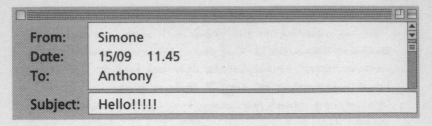
Dear Anthony,

Hi there on Blue Power Ranger Ward. As you can see, we do have e-mail. It's great, isn't it? I love e-mailing all my friends but I'm not allowed to go on any chat lines in case of perverts and I can't stay on for ever because of the ££$$£££. We got it during the summer. Jem, my mum's partner, needs it to find acting work because he's resting at the moment. Resting is the word actors use when they're unemployed. My dad laughed when he heard that—he said he might have guessed they weren't sponging like the rest of them. You could say Dad's not a big lover of the acting profession, apart from Bruce Willis, especially now he has to pick me up from extra technology class on his Cash and Carry night. Jem can't do it because he had to sell his van to pay for the Internet and Mum's at college so she can't do it either. Alexis, Dad's girlfriend, did offer but Mum said she wasn't having me driven home by someone who was that stupid she thought four star was the name of a pop group. As you can tell, things are as complicated as ever at my end. In fact, they're mega-complicated but that's another story.

Anyway, read what you put about the card. I'm sorry you didn't like it but just shove it behind the others on your cabinet, like I suggested. It is the thought that counts, though, isn't it?

OK, gotto go—have got stacks of work to do. I'm glad I'm only in top set for English and not for everything like you—I couldn't cope—especially with German to learn as well. I don't know why we have to start learning a second foreign language when we've only just started learning a first, do you?

By the way, you weren't serious about doing homework in hospital, were you??

Simone

From: Anthony
Date: 16/09   08.33
To: Simone
Subject: Homework Details

Excellent news about the e-mail. Didn't think you'd have it what with living in a council house and coming from a broken home. First of all, don't worry—I won't inundate you with trivia during our correspondence—I'm sure you receive enough of that from your dipsy girlfriends such as Chloe S. and Tamla K. *My* e-mails will be totally professional, concerned only with educational matters. I was surprised at your comment about not doing homework just because I am in hospital, S. You are *aware* there are only 88 revision weeks left to the SATs in Year 9? I cannot afford to allow my standards to slip merely because I had a near death experience.

I believe my mother is going to contact your mother about bringing work home for me anyway but you can e-mail it to me now directly. She'll probably contact you about the delivery of textbooks and so on.

Make sure the homework instructions are crystal clear, won't you? I'd hate to get anything wrong. German's an absolute doddle, by the way. I don't know what you're fussing about.

Before I sign off, I have to say I found your comments on the card rather disappointing, even patronizing—*it's the thought that counts?* Come on, S, we both know 8DC haven't got the power of thought without me. Talk about pass the brain cell. No, I stand by what I said, the card was pitiful and they must do better. Please relay my feelings to them so they can make amends by choosing a suitable gift.

ABB

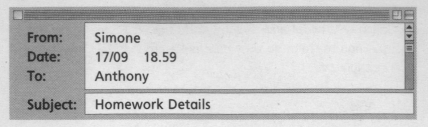

From:	Simone
Date:	17/09 18.59
To:	Anthony
Subject:	Homework Details

Dear Anthony,

Your mum has just phoned (she was on for the whole of *Emmerdale* and well into *West Country Today*). It was funny hearing her voice, not because she's got a funny voice but because hearing her brought back loads of memories from primary school, some of them good, some of them not so good. Mrs Bent (your mum, obviously) was not exactly my favourite teacher, no offence.

Will be in touch when I've gathered all your homework and stuff from the teachers. I will do it this week, but I am a bit stressed at the moment, so if you could ask Olly for next time, I'd appreciate it. He is your best bud and it would be miles easier for him to do it seeing as he's a brainiac like you and in all the top sets. (Is that being patronizing? I had to look it up and it said 'condescending' so I had to look that up, too, and it said 'being patronizing' so I got confused. Whatever it means, I can tell it's not a compliment, so you must be feeling better!!!)

Oh yeah—why did you have to panic me about SATs in 88 weeks time when I can't even get through today's homework? To think this time last year, as a new Year Seven, all I was worried about was how I would get to

know all the teachers' names and if I would ever get to chew a flapjack at break-time because the queue in the canteen was so massive and stuff like that. Now I have so many things going round my brain, some of them in German, that I think it might blow up any second. True, a lot of the things in my brain are small things, like homework, homework, homework, and homework but some of them are big things. The big things are private, though, so I'm not going to tell you them. You're not exactly the best person in the world to tell personal stuff to, no offence.

Right—must go or I won't have time to write to my 'dipsy' friends. Chloe's not one of them, by the way—she doesn't talk to me much now that she has discovered boys, smoking, and padded bras.

Simone

I'm sorry it seems to be such a big problem for you to undertake the simple act of collecting homework for a classmate in hospital. Thought it would be obvious why we've asked you to forward my homework: a) you are fairly reliable; b) as the school, lamentably, only streams for English, Maths, and French, we are in the same groups for all other subject areas such as IT, music, etc.; c) Oliver Woodman's a big creep and I wouldn't ask him a favour if he was the last Year Eight in the universe. Hope that's clear enough—don't go turning into an airhead like all the other girls, S.

Incidentally, what was that supposed to mean: 'you're not exactly the best person in the world to tell personal stuff to'? Compared to whom? That awful Melanie McCleod the convict's daughter or your neighbourhood chum Peter Bacon, whose family look as if they have just finished starring in a remake of *Dumb and Dumber*? Honestly!

So, any news on the collection for the 'get well soon' present?

ABB

Subject: The Truth

Dear Anthony,

Your last e-mail was really rude. I've got enough going on round here without finding stuff like that in my in-box when I come home, you know. I don't even know why you have to be so snide about my friends in the first place—they've never done anything to you. I think there's one or two things I need to tell you, Anthony. I wasn't going to because you are poorly but I reckon if you're well enough to dish it out you're well enough to get some back. Here goes.

The Truth About The Card

Well, I suppose it was a bit 'pitiful' and if it had been me receiving it I would have been upset, too, but it took me ages to get anyone to write anything decent at all. Also, it wasn't Peter who wrote Eileen Dover or Ivor Bigbutt on the card, it was me. I was just trying to cheer you up and use up the spaces at the same time. While we are on the subject of Peter, it's only Luther who lets the Bacon family down, Anthony. Mr and Mrs Bacon are really nice and Peter and his two younger sisters are almost normal since they've been put on Ritalin, so what you said about *Dumb and Dumber* was totally out of order.

While I'm at it, you know how your mum came in to

11

complain about us being heartless because nobody helped you when you were writhing in agony during drama? As Mr Welch explained, how were we supposed to know your appendix had just splattered—sorry—ruptured? We thought you were still being sarcastic when you began jigging about on the floor. I don't know whether you can remember or not but you had

been saying things like, 'Ooh, look out, Julia Roberts and Tom Cruise,' to every group during presentation time, or else you just did that sneery thing with your lip and went: 'Was that *it*?' That's not the best way to get sympathy, you know.

Perhaps you need to work on your **people skills** so that next time another organ bursts inside you someone will call an ambulance instead of shouting, 'Get up, you dozy plank.' (Mr Welch says he does regret saying that now, with hindsight.)

So there!

Simone

PS: Writing Simone instead of S all the time would be a start!

From: Anthony
Date: 19/09   08.10
To: Simone
Subject: The Truth (??)

Dear SIMONE

Pardon me for asking but what are people skills when they are at home? Just thought I'd better know before I respond to your crass accusations.

  ABB

From: Simone
Date: 19/09   16.45
To: Anthony

Subject: People Skills

<u>People Skills: an explanation for those in need</u>
I learned the term 'people skills' from my dad's girlfriend, Alexis. Alexis has been on a course at Bartock Business College (BBC) to learn all about people skills and VAT. You need both to run a shop successfully. Alexis and her friend Toni opened a costume hire shop last Saturday above Dad's newsagents. As you probably guessed from the headed notepaper I attached to your get-well card, the shop is called *'Stars in Your Size'* (get it, like the TV programme *Stars in Your Eyes*? Melanie McCleod and I thought of it and the caption about

disguises and sizes. I think it's clever but I guess you'll think it's rubbish).

I could ask Alexis for her people skills course notes, if you're interested. On second thoughts, I won't ask her just yet, though, because she's stressed out and everything's a 'nightmare'. One of her big problems is her special promotion. If you spend over £25 on costume hire in the first week you get either a false hairy chest or a Tina Turner-cum-Rod Stewart wig absolutely free. It was supposed to be a once-in-a-lifetime offer. The promotion went in the *Bartock Post* and they sent a photographer and everything. The trouble was, the hairy chests never arrived and the wigs looked like dead guinea pigs and nobody wanted one.

Now look what I'm doing. I'm giving away too much about my personal life—I always end up doing that. It's a good job I'm not allowed on any chat lines or our telephone bill would be about three million pounds a quarter.

Anyway, in a nutshell, you don't have many people skills, Master Bent, and that's why you got a pitiful card and that's why nobody's collecting for a present for you, either. Sorry if that's a shock to you but you might as well know now. I did try but even people like Anna Trevelyn and Martin Magilton were coming out with things like 'no chance' or 'why should I?' when I asked for a donation and they go to church, so that tells you something. Sorry, but there it is.

Simone

Well, thank you for putting me straight on so many things, SIMONE. And all this time I was thinking it was just good manners to send a small greeting card and a simple gift to a child in hospital. How misguided I was. Well, you can rest assured I won't bother you again. I wouldn't want to inflict my unwanted presence upon any of you: church goers, atheists, agnostics, and pagans alike, for a moment longer than necessary. I'll inform mother she must make other arrangements about homework etc. and I will ask for a transfer to another class upon my return to Bartock High. I just hope it doesn't cause Mummy too much distress by bringing back memories of when I was bullied in Year Seven and she had to transfer me from Alabaster Boys to Bartock High mid way through. You probably don't remember that rather dark period in my life but I shall probably need therapy for it during my twenties. Still, you don't want to know about my problems, do you, when you have so many of your own?

Incidentally, before I terminate all contact, I do not do a 'sneery' thing with my lip, nor am I in need of 'people skills', thank you very much, nor am I in <u>any way</u> bad at listening. In fact, I am an excellent listener, after years of practice on my parents' telephone extension, so if you had wanted to share your problems with me rather than the daughter of a man with connections to the underworld, you could have done so in confidence, though worrying about your father's girlfriend's hairy chest situation is hardly a 'big' problem, if you want my opinion.

Anyway, I'll go now. I won't ever disturb you again, or offer to help you with your German homework as I was going to once my stitches had knitted fully.

Yours sincerely,

Anthony Beaumont Bent ex-8DC

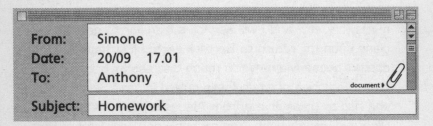

From:	Simone
Date:	20/09　17.01
To:	Anthony

| Subject: | Homework |

Here's your homework, Anthony. I know you'll enjoy it.

Look, let's just forget about the last couple of e-mails, shall we? I talked it through with my mum and she says being in hospital can make people feel a bit tetchy and isolated and I do know how that feels so I guess I'll carry on collecting your homework for you until you're better. I admit I had forgotten about the bullying at Alabaster Boys but I still think you could cut back on the sarcasm this end. There's definitely no need to get transferred to another class or anything drastic like that. Anyway, 8DC has got a better reputation than loads of the other Y8s and Mr Curbishley's just got to be the best form tutor ever. Who else would say 'nice shot' when someone pukes on their Nubuck shoes by accident like Clifford Hammond did in Year Seven? Besides, we're working together for IT. Miss Brighton has put you in a group with me, Chloe, and Peter for this term. I guess you won't be too thrilled about it but at least you'll miss most of the lessons—I won't. I'll be stuck with Chloe going on about how many boys she snogged at the youth club the night before. Urgh!

I think you'll like the topic though. We've got to design a series of web pages for Year 8, the best of which will go on to the school's actual website—all the details are in the attachment. Let me have your ideas ASAP.

Simone

PS: My problems aren't to do with Alexis, by the way, they're to do with my mum.

So relieved you have relented, S. (am returning to S for sake of speed—OK?)

Have done the homework, such as it was. I finished it in about an hour. I do wish they would stretch us more, don't you? I don't know how many times mother has been in to the Head about it.

I liked the IT from Miss Brighton, though. Designing web pages is so obviously my forte. My father, as you probably know, is an executive website consultant currently working on highly important material in the United States of America. His project is so important, he couldn't fly back to me, even in my darkest hour. Doing this project well for Miss Brighton will show him how clever I am, too.

Here is my plan—just forward it to Miss B. No need to show it to CS or PB—hardly think they'd be capable of understanding it anyway. Can you ask Miss B if we're using JPEG or GIF for the imaging so I know how much compression power we'll have? Our pixel count is highly important when deciding on the pictures we are going to use.

YEAR 8 WEB PAGES
Please Read Carefully

Plan: 12 pages using HTML compatible to whichever crummy system the school currently has. We'll use relative links and absolute links to create our pages with hierarchic rather than basic linear structure leading back to the homepage.

Suggested topics:

☞ Revision tips—it's never too soon to start—this could be an interactive page with e-mail options for those who want personalized advice from someone who has applied for membership of Mensa.

☞ enjoyable mathematical investigations by Anthony Bent

☞ how to find your way around a forest or moor without a compass

☞ Sports results

☞ Book page—Anthony's recommendations for advanced readers including an essay on the country's greatest contemporary writer of children's fiction, Mr Philip Pullman

☞ Current issues of importance to Y8s (I'm thinking lack of equipment in the gym, extending the curriculum to include Latin and/or Greek, greater access to careers advice, and elocution lessons for the more appalling regional dialects among the teaching staff to name but a few . . .)

All Ideas By ABB WEBMASTER 8DC
(Other members of group: Simone Wibberley, Chloe Shepherd, Peter Bacon)

PS: Didn't realize you were having problems with your mother. I'm not having the best of times with mine, to be honest. She's got an Ofsted inspection coming up at her school and seems to be giving that far more attention than me, her desperately ill only child, so you see, I do understand. I presume your problems with your mother are something to do with her lifestyle. Has she turned to drink or drugs to forget? Or has she run up scores of credit-card debts by being allowed to borrow heavily from agencies who prey on women with low incomes? You can tell me, S. I remember her from the school gates before divorce and heroin ravaged her attractive features.

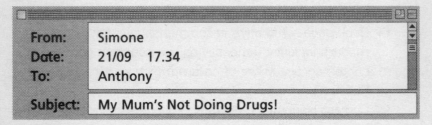

From:	Simone
Date:	21/09 17.34
To:	Anthony
Subject:	My Mum's Not Doing Drugs!

Anthony—what are the nurses putting in your soup? Of course my mum's not doing drugs, you dummy! My mum's in the final year of her physiotherapy course and I'm dead proud of her for going back to college and making something of her life. You might see her in the out-patients one day, if she gets to the out-patients stage now, because she's having a baby. That's what my problem is. Sorry it's not more interesting than that—for you, anyway. It's a huge thing for me.

To be honest, I'm not sure how I feel about it, especially as Mum isn't happy—she thinks she's too old to go through all that again (she's 35). Jem's younger

(33) and has never been through it, so he's thrilled to bits. It means I don't know whether to be happy or sad, depending on who I'm with, so it's all a bit confusing. Anyway, now you know. My baby brother or sister is due some time in February. It's about as big as a grapefruit at the moment, which is a weird thought.

   Feel free to make fun like Chloe Shepherd will when she finds out.

<u>Simone</u>

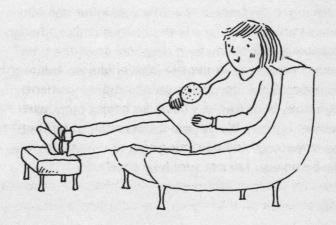

From: Anthony
Date: 21/09   18.21
To: Simone
Subject: Siblings

I think it's super news about the baby and don't know why you were making such a deal out of it. Of course your mother's not too old. My mother was 41 when she had me and I turned out to be of well above average intelligence with few blemishes, apart from a slight over-bite and tendency towards dry skin.

I often wish I had brothers or sisters. That would take the pressure off me having to succeed all the time and carry on the Bent name all alone. I quite envy the others on the ward during visiting time, though some of the younger siblings are far too noisy and out of control.

Have you thought of names, yet?

I think Miles is a suitable first name for a boy, possibly William. Both would go with Wibberley. Elisabeth with an 's' for a girl. Or Antonia. If you're looking for something unusual and strong, Lyra is the obvious choice, though I was saving that for my own daughter when the time came. I expect you're already making lists or, knowing you, designing a cot that rocks non-stop or something.

Speaking of design, you won't let all this baby stuff prevent you from giving your full attention to the web pages, will you? What did you think of the ideas? How impressed was Miss Brighton by them?

ABB

Dear Anthony,

Thanks for what you said about the baby—I thought you might think it was disgusting so it was nice of you to say you think it is OK. It's such a relief being able to talk about it to someone. Only Mel knows at school—I haven't even told Tamla yet, and she's my best friend.

The thing was, Mum was so dumbstruck when she first found out, she wouldn't talk about it at all and made Jem and me swear we wouldn't mention it outside the house. She was in a mardy for weeks and still hasn't begun blooming properly like you're supposed to. She keeps saying things like: 'What about my career? It's over before it's even begun, isn't it?', and: 'Where are we going to get the money from?', and: 'Where are we going to put it?' (the baby, not the money) and other things I can't repeat because I know you come from a non-swearing background.

In fact, I can hear Mum downstairs now, going on and on. I'm glad I'm going to Dad's for the weekend. Poor Jem!

Hope it's quieter your end.

Simone

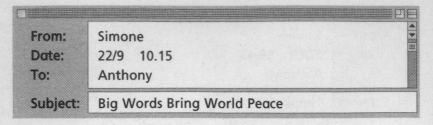

From:	Simone
Date:	22/9 10.15
To:	Anthony
Subject:	Big Words Bring World Peace

Just have to tell you this. You know I've just said Mum and Jem were having a row about the baby while I was writing to you? Well, when I got downstairs it was turning into something a bit too serious and I began to get really worried in case they split up. I've been through that once and I'm not going through it again so I yelled at them both. I went: 'Pack it in you two—at once !!!' Mum stopped mid-flow because I don't back-chat my parents like some people I could mention, so I took advantage of the shocked silence and followed up quickly with, 'You're both so puerile.' That's one of your words, isn't it? Anyway, that seemed to do the trick because they looked at me, then each other, then started laughing.

So, even though you are miles away in hospital, Anthony, your wide vocabulary has helped my family because they both sat down and had a proper talk with tea and Jaffa cakes. In the end, Jem announced he'll be a house husband so that Mum can go straight back to college when the baby's born and then she can look for a job once she qualifies. He promised he'd stay at home even if he's offered the starring role in a Hollywood film opposite Nicole Kidman for fifty million dollars (that was my question to test him). Jem keeps his promises, so now Mum's over the moon, too.

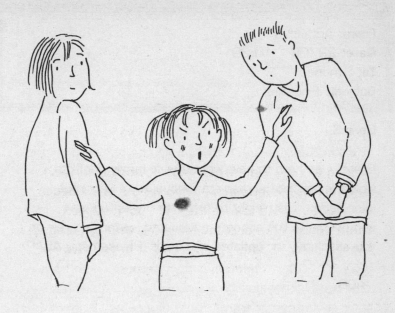

Anyway, gotta go—Dad'll be here any minute and he hates it if I'm not ready and waiting because it means he has to make small-talk with Mum and Jem and it gets awkward. Mum's even leaving it up to me to tell Dad about the baby, they're that rubbish at one-to-one.

Oh, by the way, I liked some of the names you chose but the baby won't be a Wibberley, remember, it will be a Cakebread like Jem or a Cakebread-Fiddy because Fiddy was my mum's maiden name and she would use that, not her slave name (that's what she calls her married name). It might even just be a Fiddy because Mum and Jem aren't married or anything. You can see how complicated life is for children of divorced people.

Oh well. Gotta really go. Smell you later.

25

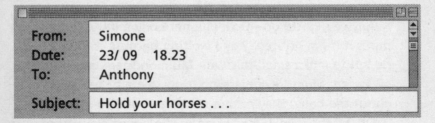

From: Anthony
Date: 22/09   10.30
To: Simone
Subject: Priorities

Dear S,

Grateful as I am to have solved your family conflicts
would appreciate immediate feedback on web page
information. Distraught to discover my laptop isn't
compatible to the school's antiquated system so rely on
you absolutely for updates and input. Please reply ASAP.

   ABB

From: Simone
Date: 23/ 09   18.23
To: Anthony

Subject: Hold your horses . . .

Dear Anthony,

Haven't even handed stuff in yet!! Will see Miss
Brighton tomorrow at break especially, OK?
   How'd your weekend in hospital go? Do they still do
those ice-cream sundae things with chopped nuts and
green cherries on top as a Saturday treat? I used to love
those.
   It was OK at Dad's. I spent most of my time helping

Alexis with the costumes in the shop but there wasn't much to do apart from check for stains and tears. September's a slack month for parties, apparently, but she's hopeful for Hallowe'en.

I told Dad about the baby. He thought I was kidding at first. 'How far along is she?' he asked, testing me out. I said I wasn't sure but I knew the baby was a bit bigger than a grapefruit at the moment. Then he just snorted and said, 'Ha! So much for "Miss I Need My Space" ' which wasn't the most supportive reaction ever. Alexis didn't snort or even smile. She just looked blank and said she had more to worry about than things like babies. I think she was in a mardy because someone had returned her only Captain Kirk outfit with a cigarette burn under the armpit.

Anyway, homework time. Urghhh!!!!

Simone

From: Anthony
Date: 23/09   20.03
To: Simone
Subject: trivia

Don't quite seem to be making myself clear. Not exactly bothered about ice-cream sundaes and Captain Kirk's armpits. Just update me on what happens at break vis-a-vis web pages ASAP.

ABB

From:	Simone
Date:	24/09 17.58
To:	Anthony

Subject:	Web Stuff

Dear Anthony,

<u>Sorry, sorry—web page stuff. Right.</u>

Miss Brighton said we would never get twelve pages done when I showed her your planning sheet but understands your need to be stretched, so to limit it to a simple six, though still only one page, or possibly two, will go on the actual website if it is chosen. Only our group and Olly Woodman's group is being allowed to go for six pages. The good news for you is that Chloe, Pete, and me thought we would definitely go with your idea about a sports page because sport is popular with a lot of pupils at Bartock High and your idea of books because we have got Book Week coming up in October, so that's two sorted already. We'll do the rest in IT on Thursday—we're all into this topic, by the way, so there's no need to worry about us letting you down or anything.

Mrs Jagger is very excited about Book Week because she has managed to get the children's writer Gillian Cross, who wrote the Demon Headmaster stories that were on TV, to come for one of the days. Mrs Jagger went straight to the top this year because the poet they had last year swore a lot during the workshops which is the last thing you want when you're next door to the RE department. (If you can think of any questions to ask a visiting author, let me have them ASAP as I am in charge of that page. It makes sense, with me being a library helper on Tuesday and Thursday lunchtimes.)

Chloe volunteered to take charge of the sports page. I was a bit surprised at first because she's never been very sporty but then I found out she fancies Olly. Apparently she's only attracted to boys who look as if they 'work-out' this year. I said 'Does that mean gardeners and refuse collectors?' but she didn't get it and just replied flatly, 'It means Oliver Woodman so keep your hands off.' As if I care who she goes out with. Why did you call him a creep, by the way? I think he's OK. Did something happen during the summer? You were always riding past my house on your bikes.

Simone

From: Anthony
Date: 24/09   18.22
To: Simone
Subject: Web Pages

Your news is grave indeed. Am alarmed by fact that
Woodman's group also being stretched. Pardon me if I
don't share your high opinion of him but I have my private
reasons. We must not let that creep take advantage of
my absence. Update on web pages and any other
homework needed very, very quickly. If Shepherd and
Bacon insist on involvement I want to approve their
'ideas' so we can get on with it. If they're as 'into it' as
you say I don't see why you all have to wait until IT on
Thursday to complete your ideas. Couldn't you meet
during lunch instead of stacking books or whatever it is
you all do?

Response within the hour would be appreciated.

A

From:	Simone
Date:	24/09 19.55
To:	Anthony
Subject:	Web Pages

Yes, sir! Will get on to it straight away, sir!

From: Anthony
Date: 24/09   20.08
To: Simone
Subject: Web Pages

And I'm the sarcastic one?

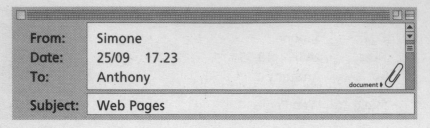

From:	Simone
Date:	25/09 17.23
To:	Anthony
Subject:	Web Pages

All right, Anthony, you can stop panicking now, here they are—the rest of our ideas delivered to you faster than you can say *homework sucks*.

 As you can see, we've all come up with loads of ideas, so that's proof of our commitment. Chloe's on report (for fighting with Josephine Lyons in the changing rooms. They were fighting over a Y9 they both fancy— how pathetic) so anyway, she has to be committed or she gets done but even you have got to be impressed by Pete's list—he's written a whole page full of things, which is a miracle for him. Trouble is, we couldn't decide what to choose from every list to get it down to six web pages so have decided to have votes. You can have four votes, one for each page left, but you are not allowed to vote for your own ideas. I don't want to influence you but please bear in mind Miss Brighton did say we should try to make the pages have broad appeal to everyone and not just one narrow group. Her examples were Yeovil Town or Bristol City-stroke-Rovers football clubs, mine are girls who are obsessed with boys-stroke-make-up-stroke-diets.

 Simone

 PS: Questions for Gillian Cross ASAP.

From: Anthony
Date: 25/09   19.30
To: Simone
Subject: Voting

Thought majority of ideas lacking in merit so can only give my support to two. Especially surprised at yours, S. For someone usually quite inventive there was little to go on. Will not even comment on Streaky Bacon's 'miraculous' suggestions as am not supposed to laugh heavily in case burst stitches. What a bozo. He really is a moron.

My two votes are as follows:

1. Creative Writing page (SAW)
2. Investigation (CMS) but not bullying or dinners (yawn, yawn). Suggest into lack of satisfactory cloakroom facilities at Bartock High School or refer back to my original suggestions on expanding curriculum to include more worthy subjects to study.

Questions for Gillian Cross:

1. How much money do you earn per annum as a writer?
2. Have you ever met Philip Pullman, author of such masterpieces as *The Subtle Knife* and *The Amber Spyglass*? If so, when?
3. Do you know where I could send my book, *The Golden Spyglass*, when I have finished it? I could let you see the first fifteen chapters when you visit if I am off the danger list by then. (I'll let you explain to her, S)

ABB

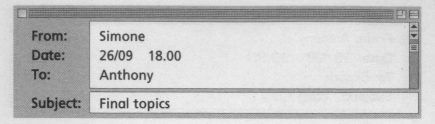

From: Simone
Date: 26/09 18.00
To: Anthony

Subject: Final topics

Dear Anthony,

Here is the final selection of topics for our web pages—sorry it's taken so long but we do have other lessons, too, you know. Our six topics for our six pages are:

1) **Sports** (your suggestion)
2) **Books** (your suggestion)
3) **Creative Writing** (my suggestion)
4) **Problem Page** (my suggestion)
5) **10 Things you need by your bedside at all times in case of attack** (Pete's)
and 6) **How2 tell if your guy or gal is right 4U and how 2 dump them if they're not** (Chloe's—of course)

We are getting cracking on these straight away. As you can't come to school just yet, there isn't much you can do to help but we will let you know what is going on. If you have a poem or a short extract from your book for the Creative Writing page you could send that to us. We are a bit behind Olly's group but nothing to get in a mardy about. I've already sent your questions off to Gillian Cross, along with ours. Mrs Jagger made me take out the one about how much money she earns, though, as that's an impertinent question, not a friendly one.

PS: You're starting with the nastiness again, Anthony. Stop calling Pete names like bozo or moron. Why do you do it? He can't help being a slow learner—not everyone's intelligent like you.

From: Anthony
Date: 26/09   20.55
To: Simone
Subject: Final Topics

Hello!! Polite Reminder!! I am ill in a hospital bed, you know. Getting really fed up with being criticized, especially where Bacon's concerned. Why are you always so over-sensitive when I come out with a bit of harmless name-calling? Do you love him or something? I will tell you why I do it, though. Because everyone's like you, feeling sorry for him and falling over backwards to help him because he's got 'special needs'. Well, I've got 'special needs', too, but no one helps me. I work hard to get my grades—they don't just materialize out of thin air, you know, but does anyone make a fuss of me? Oh no. I submit a 40-page project on Henry V111 and sure, I get an A but that's it. Peter Bacon copies two sentences and traces a picture and it's *'Have a headmaster's award, sonny'*!!

Ironically, it's just as bad at home.

I know you must yearn to be like me and live in a private house with views of the deer park but you have no idea of the pressure I'm under, especially since I dropped out of Alabaster Boys. When I got my report last year, with fourteen As and a B, guess what my father said? 'Rather let the side down with that B, Anthony. A B from a comprehensive won't get you into Oxbridge, you know.'

I'd like to clear something else up, too, now that my dander's up, Wibberley.

Don't think for <u>one minute</u> that just because I'm not in school it means you can leave me out of major decision-making activities by trying to fob me off with suggesting I send in a bit of creative writing. My creative writing is very personal, thank you very much, and I am <u>not</u> going to have it bandied about by amateurs. In short, no, I will <u>not</u> send you any of my novel and I want to know <u>everything</u> you do concerning the web pages.

Oh, and while I'm at it, you think you've got family problems, do you? What about me? Imagine being in hospital with only one visitor for half an hour per evening. Mummy has now limited her visiting time because she's got the inspectors in at Woodhill Primary in two weeks (if you remember) and there's 'so much' to do in her classroom beforehand. It's amazing how quickly *her* attention has returned to displays on pollination and water cycles now that I am no longer at death's door.

Father e-mails me every day but only to update me on *his* news. I asked him to send me ideas for creating the best web page ever but he said I had to do it myself because he hasn't time for distractions. As usual there, too. You'd think they'd show a bit more concern for their only child, wouldn't you?

It's not as if I've got hundreds of friends, either. I think sometimes I should have been less selective like you and befriended anyone and everyone rather than concentrating on one person of almost equal intelligence like Oliver Woodman. Yes, we did spend nearly the whole summer on our bikes exploring, if you must pry, but I suppose you've guessed by now we had a massive falling-out towards the end of the holidays over something totally trivial.

I feel as if nobody cares about me at all.

ABB

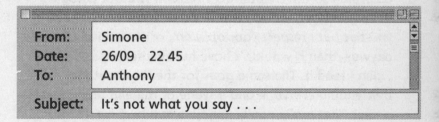

From: Simone
Date: 26/09 22.45
To: Anthony

Subject: It's not what you say . . .

Dear Anthony,

It's way past my bedtime but your last e-mail kept going round and round my mind and I couldn't sleep so Mum's letting me write this at this time just this once.

You're doing it again, Anthony! Being really horrible. If it wasn't for the last bit you put about nobody caring I would definitely not be writing back to you. People do care, it's just—I don't know—like Mum says to me sometimes when she thinks I've got a bad attitude—she gives me a look and says, 'You know why I'm cross, Simone, it's not *what* you said, it's the *way* you said it.'

You do that too. You say things wrong, Anthony. You always have and I've been with you since Reception Class so I should know. Maybe you don't mean it but it comes out nasty and it's nothing to do with other people being over-sensitive, it's you that's under-sensitive. I suppose I can see why you get fed up if you don't feel you get enough reward for your hard work but you still don't need to take it out on everyone else. I don't just mean Peter, either. You do it to me, too. e.g: When you put things like: 'Do your research, Simone, *it's a basic*' and you underline for emphasis. What you could have said, according to the chapter on 'Phrasing without Enraging' in *People Skills*, level 1, was: '*I don't agree with what you put but I respect your opinion*', or something close, anyway, then it wouldn't have hurt my feelings so much when I read it. The same goes for the bit about me befriending *everyone* and *anyone* at the end of the last e-mail. That really, really annoyed and hurt me. It felt like you were saying I was desperate or common or something. I asked Mum if befriending was a bad thing and she said it was a great thing and to keep it up. I could go on, Anthony, but I guess you'll get my point.

No one's trying to leave you out of the web pages work, either, but if you're not here when we make our decisions, it's not our fault, is it? We'll never get anything done if we have to come back to you for your opinion every time, especially as you'll only contradict everything we say. We'd be way behind every group, not just Olly's.

I talked all this over with my mum because I was upset about it. My mum thinks you sound like an unhappy child and that your unhappiness shows itself by being spiteful and sarcastic. She reckons your sarcasm is a defence mechanism. I asked her what one of those was when it was at home and she says it's what you do to protect yourself, like when hedgehogs curl up if they sense danger. I said the last time I saw you, you were curled up like a hedgehog but I didn't think it was a mechanism. More like a mecha-spasm. (Sorry, that was a really bad joke—I take after my dad, joke-wise.) My mum wants to know if you want her to say anything to your mum about lengthening her visits to you or something if she phones again?

I'm collecting your next lot of homework. I'll attach it after IT tomorrow or Friday at the latest. Meanwhile, why don't you write to us at school? If everyone knew how you felt underneath they might be nicer. Or you could write to Olly. Whatever you fell out about can't have been that bad and he does seem a bit fed up lately but that could be because of Chloe pestering him.

Simone

Dear Simone,

Perhaps I could tone it down a little. You are not the first to comment on my sharp tongue. I will try to modify my phrasing in future.

Is it really true that Oliver looks fed up without me? If it is, I'll perhaps write to him but if you're just saying it to coax me, I shan't bother and I don't really feel up to writing to 8DC just yet. However, I am looking forward to receiving my homework.

Tell your mother it was kind of her to worry but ask her not to mention any of this to my mother as she doesn't like fussy children. It must be nice to be able to discuss things so freely with a parent, even if your mother does seem to over-analyse. Defence mechanism? I don't think so.

<u>Web pages</u>

I feel happier now that you have told me you are not excluding me deliberately but I would appreciate being kept up to date on progress. I can tell you how to make blinking captions and create links to other sites if you've got the text ready. And we really must finalize the contents so I can start on the menu and headers. Left hand side for scrolling, I believe is best. Have a look at the choice of buttons under 'menu'. I suggest something bold such as yellow arrows on black circular background.

Do avoid choosing something 'gimmicky' and whatever you do, refresh at all times (only a suggestion, of course, from someone with the most experience).

I am going to start putting *actions* where the website is concerned. It will guide you as to my needs in a simple, not-spiteful-at-all way. Here are my first ones:

Actions

1. send me finalized list of contents
2. decide on menu buttons and let me know ASAP (please).

Anthony

PS: I would never think of you as common or desperate.

From:	Simone
Date:	27/09 19.23
To:	Anthony
Subject:	Letter coming

Got your e-mail. It was miles better in attitude. Keep it up, as Mr Pikelet always puts at the end of our English work. Homework and news on its way.

Simone

From: Anthony
Date: 27/09   19.56
To: Simone
Subject:

Thank you.

Anthony

Dear Anthony,

Here's your homework, just in time for the weekend as promised. If you're wondering why there isn't much, it is because three teachers have been away on courses. Mr English has given us a mountain of German and French, though. Tamla and I think Mr English has been to teachers' boot camp during the summer holidays because he's changed from a nervous new teacher when we had him in Y7 into the strictest one ever. He doesn't take any nonesense. e.g. yesterday in German he was teaching us names for members of the family and he nearly gave us a class detention just because everyone laughed when he told us *vater*, which means father, is pronounced *farter*. I admit Pete didn't help by saying, 'That sums my dad up—he's the best *vater* in the world' over and over again just as we tried to settle, but teachers need to see the funny side of things as well as having good control. Maybe it takes years before they can do both at once.

Sorry, but Miss Brighton was one of those teachers on a course so we couldn't do any more to the website in the lesson, mainly because the supply teacher said he didn't know one end of a computer from another so there was no point even switching them on. I'll show her your letter when we have her next time, though, to help with the computer language you use. We haven't done blinking captions or blinking text links or very blinking much really so we can't do any of your 'actions' yet. We've started collecting our data in our spare time, though. I'm asking everyone for their problems and am waiting patiently for Gillian Cross to reply, Pete's compiling his list of 10 things, and Chloe's still following Olly round at lunchtimes, pretending she's interviewing him for the sports page. She makes it so obvious she fancies him. In fact everything about Chloe Madelaine Shepherd is so obvious. Obvious and shallow.

On the subject of ex-friends, I don't know why you fell out with Olly but I did tell him you were bored and I also said lonely. Even though you only said bored, I can tell you are a bit of both so I said it. He kind of shrugged and looked sort of sympathetic but said you'd have to make the first move, so it's up to you, OK?

Whatever happened between you must be pretty serious because Olly's not the sort to bear grudges. Not like Chloe. I think you should make the first move, Anthony, if you want my opinion. Everyone needs friends, especially when they've not got many to choose from.
   I know I found *mine* useful today.

   Cheers

   Simone

From: Anthony
Date: 28/09   18.30
To: Simone
Subject: What homework??

S—the attachment didn't arrive for some reason. Please try again promptly (it's the paperclip icon). You sound a teeny bit annoyed with Chloe—has she been favouring you with her version of sarcasm again by any chance?

   A.

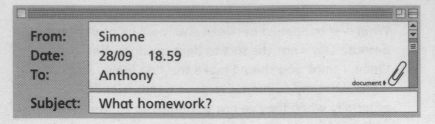

Ooops! I've tried again with your homework—let me
know if you don't get it this time. I must have forgotten
to click something. And no, I'm not a teeny bit annoyed
with Chloe—I'm massively and enormously annoyed with
Chloe. Thanks for noticing!!!

Somehow she found out about Mum having the baby
and she had a go at me in the dining room at
lunchtime. Guess what she said to me in front of the
whole queue? 'Well, we all know what your mum's been
doing, Simone.' So I said, 'What?' and she said, 'Well, if
you don't know, I can lend you my science book from
last year when we did sex education.' She said the word
'sex' dead loud. I knew I was going red but I just said,
'So?' and she said, 'Fancy being pregnant at her age,'
(told you she would) before sneering and adding, 'It's
disgusting.' Then Tamla chipped in and said back, 'Not
as disgusting as your face.' Chloe couldn't retort because
Mr English was buying a cheese and pickle baguette
close by so she did her snooty special instead. I don't
know why Chloe has to be such a c-o-double-u all the
time when we were best friends from Year 1 to Year 6
and bits of Y7 but if she wants to be a c-o-double-u
that's her look-out. I've got real friends like Tamla now,
thankfully. Tam didn't go into a mass strop or anything
because I hadn't told her about Mum like Chloe would

have. That's the difference between them—Tamla is strop-free. It's such a relief having a decent friend. I couldn't have outfaced Show-off Shepherd without her.

Gotta go—I'm at Dad's tomorrow so need to pack.

Hope your stitches are still knitting—perhaps they could make a jacket for the baby? (Ha! Ha!)

Simone

From: Anthony
Date: 28/09   20.58
To: Simone
Subject: Homework and baby congratulations

Dear Simone,

Thanks for the homework—it arrived this time. As you warned, there wasn't much, so I've done it all, even the German and French. Learning a foreign langauge is actually not that difficult, once you put your mind to it. If you want any help, let me know.

As for Chloe, ignore every single thing she says to you. Her parents were the bane of my mother's life when she was in Y6. Mother always said the Shepherds had too much money and not an ounce of common sense. The things I overheard on that extension that I could tell you about them were I not in a position of responsibility.

One thing you can tell her from me—the sports results

should be put into tables with columns. Make sure she refreshes/saves every move. It's a basic. Tell her also to focus on something other than Oliver. Oliver isn't the only athlete in the school, though I admit he is one of the best in our year, but not *the* best.

I've just sent him an e-mail, by the way. At first I wasn't going to but I thought about your friendship with Tamla and the positive effect it has on you, so I wrote to Oliver *and* I included an apology for our altercation during the summer. Keep this between us, Simone, but what happened was, in a fit of pique I moved the flag on the Bartock Outward Bound Summer Challenge so that he got totally lost and came in 17th instead of equal third with me. I know it sounds bad but he did push me in a bank of nettles afterwards and throw my medal in a bog so he had his revenge. It took three days for my rash to disappear. I await his reply.

Have a nice weekend.

Anthony

From:	Simone
Date:	29/09 08.00
To:	Anthony
Subject:	Olly

So that's what you fell out about. Nettles and medals.
Ouch!

I think you did the right thing to apologize. Hope you
hear back from him.

Simone

Simone—as you're still at home, I thought I'd send you my new idea for the web pages.

Ever since one of the student nurses spilt Lucozade over my *Amber Spyglass* and glucosed the pages together, I have been reading what passes for literature on this ward. In other words, piles of girls' teen magazines. (I'm beginning to see why Chloe and many others in school are so wayward. The articles are useless. I couldn't find one in-depth article on politics or any chess challenges.) I confess to being intrigued by the <u>problem pages</u> and have learned a lot more from these than I would have expected about anatomy and toiletries. In short, I think we should adopt the idea of using photographs of ourselves on our problem page and having a variety of viewpoints from different 'experts'. I'll be the homework/computer queries expert, you can be the family problems expert, Chloe the bodily functions expert, and Bacon—well, he'll just have to do the drawings or something.

<u>Actions</u>

1. Get a passport sized recent photo of CMS, yourself, and PB.

2. Send me the problems on homework/computers you have collected so far. I could give my solution then you can type it up at school. It's so frustrating my laptop isn't

compatible to the school system or I'd be able to do everything from here.

Write soon

PS: I mentioned your mother's condition to Mummy and she sends her best wishes.

Dear Anthony,

So you've been reading girls' magazines, have you? I won't mention it if you don't! I can't stand a lot of the stuff about make-up and what to do if you fancy someone but I think the problem pages are good for girls who don't have mums or friends they can talk to properly. I like the true life stories, too. Will let Chloe and Pete know about your photo idea on Monday.

Let me know what happens with Olly.

Right, gotta go brush my teeth then make sure I'm all set for Dad's. Not looking forward to it that much because Alexis's mum, Maxine, will be there too and she's a bit over-the-top. She laughs at anything and sleeps in the nude which can shock you if you forget and look up by mistake when she's going to the bathroom in the morning. Hope Dad and Alexis never get married because she'd become my grandma and I've got enough nutty grandmas as it is without adding another one!

Smell you later,

Simone

From: Anthony
Date: 29/09 09.46
To: Simone
Subject: Oliver and miscellaneous others

Simone. Just to let you know Oliver e-mailed back and he's coming to visit this afternoon! I feel as if a weight has been torn asunder from my innards. The other good news is I think I am going to be discharged either tomorrow or Monday. I simply cannot wait to get home to my own bed.

Maxine sounds appalling. It must be dreadful coming from a dysfunctional family.

Anthony

From: Anthony
Date: 29/09 15.33
To: Simone
Subject: Oliver (again)

I know you're not there but I just wanted to tell someone. Oliver's just left. His visit went OK, I think, though he didn't bring me a present or anything. Thanks for your advice. It's such a relief to be talking to him again.

Best wishes

Anthony

From: Anthony
Date: 30/09   19.00
To: Simone
Subject: I'm coming home!

Just to let you know I am definitely being discharged
tomorrow (Monday). Mother is furious as she feels it is
too soon. I sensed that she just couldn't wait for the end
of visiting time so she could dash off and finish double
mounting her haikus.

   I was a little cheered by the news that my grandmother
has kindly agreed to look after me as I enter my period
of convalescence. It means she has to

take a week off from her voluntary
work in the Oxfam shop in Bristol but
she doesn't mind.

   I only have the one grandmother.
She's not the most child-centred
person you could meet, and will
probably spend every afternoon
browsing the shopping channels for
costume jewellery, but she does make
excellent banana custard and wears
appropriate nightwear.

Anthony

Simone

Was hoping to have heard from you by now but perhaps
your server is down. It can get very busy trying to log-on
sometimes. Just to let you know I'm home now.
Grandmother due on the 18.30 from Bristol Temple
Meads. Mother has arranged for Mrs Naylor, our next
door neighbour, to sit with me until she gets back from
school. Mrs Naylor's not that keen on me since I shot
her cat with an air rifle—it was a total accident, I was
aiming for a pigeon, but would she believe me? No. She's
downstairs listening to *The Archers* and has only been up
twice to check on my health and safety.

Anthony

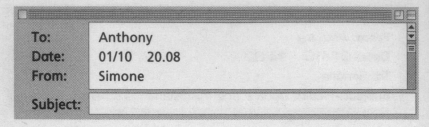

To: Anthony
Date: 01/10   20.08
From: Simone
Subject:

Dear Anthony,

The group think your idea about the problem page is OK and will bring in photos ASAP.

Simone

From: Anthony
Date: 01/10   22.09
To: Simone
Subject: !

Dear Simone,

That was a pretty short e-mail. Had totally forgotten about the photos! Great news, though. Thanks.

Anthony

From: Anthony
Date: 04/10   16.45
To: Simone
Subject: Apologies

Dear Simone

I hope you didn't think I was being sarcastic about the short e-mail. I was trying to be humorous. You haven't been in touch for days now. Web page update/ homework would be appreciated ASAP (please).

I am getting on better than I thought with grandmother. She brings me banana custard whenever I feel like it and agrees with me that my parents work too hard and has told my mother so, and my father, even though it was peak time when she made the trans-Atlantic call.

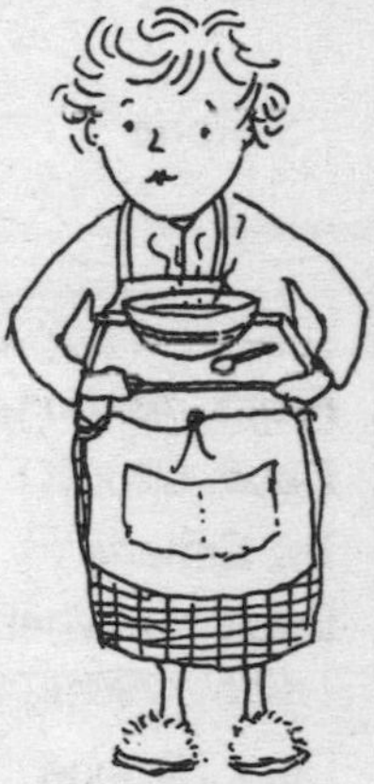

The grandmother is such a stable influence on family life, don't you think?

I hope you notice how I am trying to phrase things in a less brusque manner now. I have to admit it does seem to work with older people. I haven't had much chance to try it with my peers yet. The doctor said it will be another week at least before I can return to school.

Best wishes

Anthony

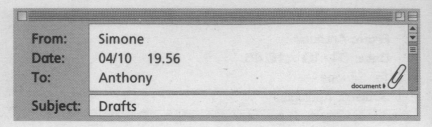

From: Simone
Date: 04/10   19.56
To: Anthony
document ▶

Subject: Drafts

Dear Anthony,

Update on web pages you asked for: I have attached our
first drafts. They include an interview with Olly, Peter's 10
things list, and three poems donated by Mr Pikelet from
his Y8 Writing Club. Chloe's still working on her 'tips'.
    You can add any comments but remember about
phrasing.

    Simone

From: Anthony
Date: 05/10   08.32
To: Simone
Subject: What's wrong?

Dear Simone

Thanks for the information but what's wrong? I have read
my past e-mails and do not think I can possibly have said
anything to offend since September 26th, apart from
perhaps describing your family as dysfunctional on
September 29th. I didn't mean dysfunctional, I meant
non-conventional in an interesting way.

    Anthony

Dear Anthony,

It's not you this time, it's me. * I don't want to talk about it. What did you think of the draft work? We still haven't heard from Gillian Cross so haven't done anything to that page. In IT, we've got as far as typing out the headers and making the menu. We chose arrow buttons that look like rotating eyeballs because they made Peter laugh the most. I have only had two genuine problems handed in so far and seventeen puerile ones but none of them were anything to do with computers or homework. A lot of the puerile ones were to do with boys having enormous body parts in certain areas, if you know what I mean.

S.

* you were right first time—my family is dysfunctional—100%

From: Anthony
Date: 05/10   21.03
To: Simone
Subject: Problems

Dear Simone,

I can tell you're not quite ready to share whatever has happened with me just yet but I'm glad you're writing again. Remember, I am no longer under-sensitive, when you do feel like confiding. For now, though, I will focus on the web pages.

   Here are my opinions.

a) Interview with OW. This is far too long.

   Action: Edit ruthlessly.

b) P. B.'s piece. As I know you like to protect him, I shall just say that although I don't agree with what he's written, (e.g. from where does the average twelve year old acquire a rocket launcher or are his family even more deranged than I suspected?) I respect his opinion.

(*People Skills, Book 1*)

c) Poems. I did see some merit in these.

Action: check in clip-art to see whether there is a picture of a manatee to go with Joshua Martin's poem.

d) I think the rotating eyeballs are a <u>big</u> mistake—too gimmicky—they will irritate after a while and take a long time to download.

Action: find an alternative.

e) You can let me have a go at the two genuine problems, if you want. I feel I have read enough magazines to qualify. In fact, I have moved on to *Good Housekeeping* and *Hello* now, thanks to my grandmother.

Best wishes

Anthony

Dear Anthony,

I haven't read *Good Housekeeping* but I always look through *Hello* and *OK* when I'm at Dad's. Your grandma could always have them delivered, if she wants.

On to your comments. Here are the group's reactions to your actions:

<u>From Pete:</u> he took your point about the rocket launcher and says he will concentrate on home-made devices. He is watching my favourite videos, *Home Alone 1* and *2*, as research. Have you seen it? It's about a boy called Kevin who gets left alone at home by mistake one Christmas and has to defend his house against two burglars called The Wet Bandits. Kevin's just brilliant at thinking up ideas to stop the baddies using only materials left lying around the house, like tarantula spiders and blow torches. I think *Home Alone*'s the best film ever made but I never watch it with Melanie. Some of the scenes could be quite upsetting for an ex-burglar's daughter.

<u>From Chloe:</u> she was not going to cut down her interview at first as she thought every word was 'so the best ever', but I managed to persuade her that *maybe* how much Olly weighed when he was born was a bit unnecessary!!

Clip art: couldn't find one of a manatee (I had to look this up—I'd never heard of it. It's a sea creature, right?) but there are six pictures of whales and dolphins. I think they'll do, don't you?

Rotating Eyeballs: We are sticking to the rotating eyeballs (no offence) but we do feel we have compromised with you. It is important to compromise (*Half way is better than no way*, p. 32, *People Skills*, level 1)

Problems.

You know you said you wanted a go at answering the genuine problems? Well, one of them is about having spots but the other is about the serious subject of bullying. No offence, Anthony, but I'm not sure you're ready yet.

Simone

You are so wrong about me not being ready! I am over-ready, like a chicken (in case you don't understand my joke, this is a play on words—over-ready instead of oven-ready?) I implore you to send me the problems.

Anthony

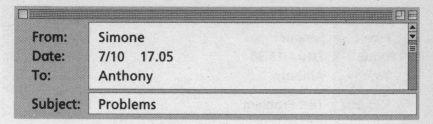

From: Simone
Date: 7/10   17.05
To: Anthony
Subject: Problems

Anthony—that oven-ready joke was foul!
OK, I'm prepared to test your People Skills development
out on a totally made-up problem first, just to see about
your phrasing and things before I let you loose on a real
one. Do you accept?

   S.

From: Anthony
Date: 7/10   17.12
To: Simone
Subject: Problem page

I accept. I am grateful for the challenge and the
opportunity to shed my under-sensitive image once and
for all.

   ABB

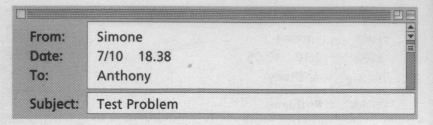

From:	Simone
Date:	7/10 18.38
To:	Anthony
Subject:	Test Problem

Here it is—beware—it's a megalongy. *Gut Gluck*!

  I am a twelve-year-old girl who stays with her father and his girlfriend at weekends. This is usually OK but last weekend I had to share my bedroom with my dad's girlfriend's mum, Maxine. Maxine was staying over because she's had a row with her third husband, Barry, and wanted a break from the deadbeat (as she called him).

  Anyway, during Sunday lunch they were all talking about my mum and her boyfriend, (they're having a baby) when Maxine said, 'I suppose you'll be spending more time with us when the baby's born.' I asked why she thought that and she said, 'Well, sugar, if this bloke's going to be at home all day with a squawking baby he won't have time for you any more, especially as you're not his real kid and the baby is. It stands to reason.' I hadn't even thought about it like that before. The baby is 100% my mum's boyfriend's and I'm 0%. The thought made me feel really sad and hurt inside. I couldn't finish my lemon meringue.

  Sad of Bartock High

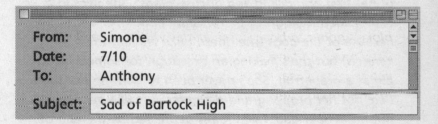

From: Anthony
Date: 7/10   19.00
To: Simone
Subject: Sad of Bartock High

Simone,

Here is my reply to the test problem. Please RSVP with your opinion ASAP.
Dear Sad of Bartock High,
Just ignore the woman. Anyone who has been married three times and sleeps in the nude should not be taken seriously.

Agony Uncle Anthony

From: Simone
Date: 7/10
To: Anthony

Subject: Sad of Bartock High

Dear Anthony,

It's not that simple, though—the girl thinks Maxine had a point. She has just let me know more details that I have passed on to you. She continues:
When I got back to my main house, things got worse. Mum's boyfriend was excited because he had felt the

*baby move and he kept saying how wonderful an experience it was and I felt really left out. I tried putting my hand on Mum's tummy but nothing happened at all. It was as if the baby didn't want anything to do with me. Then they told me Mum's boyfriend's mum, was coming down for a few days to celebrate the good news of her **first** grandchild and discuss 'plans'. She lives in a place called Moldgreen in Yorkshire and never visits because of the dogs (she doesn't like leaving them in kennels) but she's making an exception for something as big as a grapefruit. She's never been to visit me but then I am not her proper grand-daughter, just like her son is not my proper dad. I was really depressed by the end of the weekend.*

I guess my main problem is that I don't seem to fit anywhere and if I don't fit anywhere now, where will I fit when the baby's born? What if Maxine's right?

Concerned As Well As Sad of Bartock High

Dear Simone,

Agony Uncle Anthony says:
'Dear Concerned As Well As Sad of Bartock High,
** You need to talk to your mother and her partner**
about how you feel. I'm sure if they knew you were
worried they would reassure you. Otherwise, you
can always come round to my house and talk to my
mother about it but preferably after her Ofsted
inspection next week as things are becoming
increasingly tense, despite plentiful banana custard.'

  What do you think, Simone? Does this help? I thought I
was brief and straight to the point. If you get any more
probs, let me have them. I think I have found a new area
in which to excel.
  Write soon, and please don't worry,

  Anthony

From:	Simone
Date:	08/10 17.20
To:	Anthony
Subject:	Your answers

Dear Anthony,

I got your reply to the problem. This must be a first but I agree with you—you are getting better at responding in a kinder way. I thought your answer was very good indeed—I give it top marks and have attached the two genuine problems to this e-mail for you. Please reply to them and let me have them for copying up ASAP.

You were right about what you said to *Sad and Concerned of Bartock High*—the girl *should* talk to her parents about it, and usually she would but there never seems to be a right time and when the time does feel right, she can't think of the right way of putting her problem without feeling silly or sounding jealous. The girl is just going to concentrate on her German homework instead until the right moment arrives but thank you for your spot-on comments.

Best wishes

Simone

From: Anthony
Date: 08/10   20.13
To: Simone
Subject: No subject

Dear Simone

Just to let you know I received your e-mail but am not in
a mood to respond in an adequate fashion. I've managed
to compile answers to the two problems for the Problem
Page, however, as even at this most melancholy of
times, I can put others first.

A.

From: Simone
Date: 09/10   19.49
To: Anthony
Subject: Don't worry

Dear Anthony

Don't worry about not being in a replying mood. I understand. Just wait until you get the next lot of homework. You'll just be in a foul (or should that be fowl?) mood then, like me. You can tell the teachers aren't on courses this week. Thanks for the answers to the problems—I'll put them with Pete and Chloe's replies.

Gute Nacht

Simone

From: Anthony
Date: 09/10   21.49
To: Simone
Subject: Horrible Ofsted and its diabolical effect on family life

Dear Simone,

Feeling a trifle more cheerful now. We must be taking it in turns to have diabolical family dramas. I told you about mother being v.v. tense about her inspection? Well, things came to a head at teatime yesterday after mother had returned from her first day of it all. I haven't seen her as livid since Melanie McCleod put powder paint in her tea last July. Apparently the inspector only gave her lessons a 'satisfactory' but gave Mrs White *two* 'very goods' and an '*excellent*' which is like an A* at GCSE, and Mrs White has only been in the school two minutes. Mother, of course, took her bad mood out on us, ranting on and on for well over an hour about how, had she known wearing clingy cardigans and allowing children to play CDs during registration would get her top marks, she would have done it too etc. etc.

Then she actually yelled at us to keep out of her way!!!! Yelled!! In front of the aged and infirm! I ask you! I've never been so close to phoning Childline in my life.

My family may only be a small one, Simone, free from the stigma of divorce and sleazy women not wearing proper nightwear, but it is certainly far from perfect. It's going to be a long, long week, I fear.

Anthony

PS: Pray for me that mother has a good day tomorrow.

Dear Anthony,

I am sorry your mother is having a bad time at school. I am not surprised by what the inspector said (no offence) but I am surprised by her taking it out on you when she gets home. We always thought she worshipped you when we were in her class. She always seemed to give you the best marks and the most attention and the most 'Super Work' stickers. That was one of the reasons you were so unpopular. That and the sneery lip thing and the bossy attitude. It just goes to show.

   Maybe she is finding it difficult to cope while your dad is away. Why don't you e-mail and tell him what's happening?

   I've no room to talk, though. I still haven't said anything to Mum and Jem about the baby thing. I've been thinking I might just wait until the baby's born before I do or say anything. I'll have a bag packed ready, just in case, and I am already on the look out for signs, like Jem not calling me Sunshine whenever he sees me or if he tells me he hasn't time to help me with my maths homework because the baby needs changing. Things like that.

   It's funny how we are giving each other advice all the time, isn't it? A few weeks ago I would never have

written to you about my problems and you wouldn't
have written to me about yours. E-mail makes it easier
to say things to people you wouldn't say to their face, I
think.

Bye For Now

Simone

From: Anthony	
Date: 10/10 20.09	
To: Simone	
Subject: Ofsted crisis deepens	

Dear Simone,

Thanks for your last e-mail—as incisive as ever! Nothing
much to report from this end except mother's mood
hasn't improved one iota, although I can't blame her,
really. Today, after spending all those hours preparing her
Games lesson, the inspector decided to watch the Year
Fours preparing a kosher meal in RE instead. As you can
imagine, she was NOT best pleased. Grandma dashed
round to Mrs Naylor's as soon as she heard and I
headed straight to my computer. Mother's downstairs as
I write, taking her temper out on Magnus O'Puss for
pooing underneath the carport.

I can't wait to be back at school on Monday. I'll have been away for five whole weeks. I'll feel like a new student again. I'm rather anxious about it, if you must know.

Cheerio

Anthony

PS: I've been considering shortening my name to Ant in order to update my image. What do you think?

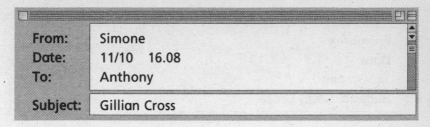

Dear Anthony

I guess I could get used to Ant instead of Anthony but it's not the best of names for shortening, is it, unless you're fond of creepy crawlies!

Guess what? I've just got back from school and found a letter from Gillian Cross. She's answered all our questions really fully and sounds really nice. She said our questions were fascinating which is a real compliment, isn't it? I've never had a letter from a proper writer before. I might get Mrs Jagger to laminate it. She's already done that for Hannah Beverley's group and their letter was only from a football manager. Anyway, it means I can also get cracking on the Book Page in IT tomorrow. Do you want me to photocopy her letter and send it to you or wait until you get back to school? You're back on Monday, aren't you? Just in time for her visit next Thursday? I think you'll be pleased with her answers to your questions but I don't want to spoil the surprise.

Must go—got to help unload the shopping from the car. I've noticed I have to do more chores these days. Mum says it's because I'm getting older but I take it as a *sign* she's training me up to take over the housework when the baby is born.

S.

From: Ant
Date: 11/10   17.11
To: Simone
Subject: Gillian Cross

Dear Simone,

Re: <u>Gillian Cross</u>
So glad to hear Gillian Cross has replied—yes, I should like a copy of her letter but there's no rush, Monday will do. It means the website pages will almost be complete, doesn't it? QUESTION: How much else is there for me to do when I return?

  Re: <u>Your Mother</u>
  Am sure your mother isn't training you for slave labour.
<u>Talk to her, Simone!</u>

  Ant (please use until further notice)

Dear Ant (I will never get used to this, Anthony!)

REPLY TO YOUR QUESTION:
There's not that much for you to do when you return.

Our only problem is we have gone way beyond Miss Brighton's limit—we're up to about twenty pages and that's without my Book Week report (oops!). I nearly died when I realized. Trouble is, what do we cut out? It's a dilemma. Maybe that's what you could do when you get back—help us snip bits out—but I would rather creep round Miss B and try to persuade her that every word is a gem.

About MUM:
Yes, I will talk to Mum but it's difficult. She's usually at college when I get in, so I do my homework, then when she gets back she does her homework, and when she's not doing the homework, she's with Jem at Parentcraft classes learning how to breathe.

Simone

Dear Simone,

Put out the flags! Mother's inspection is over, so we can all learn to breathe again in this house, too. Mummy is celebrating by having a drink of Bailey's Irish Cream liqueur or two with Grandma and Mrs Naylor in the kitchen. I must say they are being rather loud about it. I hope they don't get drunk. There's nothing worse. I seem to remember last time mother drank to excess she ended up falling asleep on the lavatory with her head resting on the toilet roll dolly. She had an imprint of the doll's face on her face the whole of the next day. It looked like a miniature gargoyle and was very unnerving. If the noise gets any louder I'll be forced to go downstairs and remind her about it, especially as Grandma has to be up at the crack of dawn to catch her train back to Bristol. I'll really miss Grandma, if not her banana custard, the daily production of which has become a little monotonous, I must admit.

The other great news is that father's contract has finished a month earlier than anticipated and he'll be

coming home next week. What with me being back at
school on Monday, everything is falling into place.

As for exceeding the limit on page numbers for the
web site, Miss Brighton can hardly complain when
students excel themselves, so I wouldn't worry about it.
I will take it upon myself to make any cuts necessary by
myself. I can be impartial and this should end your
dilemma. It's much easier for teachers' children to make
harsh decisions.

Your friend,

Ant

From:	Simone
Date:	14/10 19.33
To:	Ant
Subject:	Stuff

Dear Ant,

First of all, congratulations on having your mother back
to normal.

Second of all, wait for me in the form room at
breaktime tomorrow. We need you to write up your two
answers so we can finish the Problem Page. Don't
forget, will you? It's Room 34, in case you've forgotten
(ha! ha!) By the way, I know you were kidding about
making cuts on your own. There's no 'I' in team, you
know. (*People Skills 1, chapter 7: Team Work or Team
Jerk?*)

Anyhow, I guess this will be the last e-mail I send you
as you're back at school tomorrow and we can do
everything about the website person-to-person, but
there's some stuff we won't be able to discuss, like your
mum getting drunk!

It's weird imagining your mum drunk. Falling asleep
on the loo's not so bad, though, compared to things I've
seen. My dad's always getting drunk, especially when
we go to the Bartock Liberal Club on Saturdays. After a
few pints he goes all sloppy, or worse, starts singing.

I don't know whether he got drunk this Saturday or
not because I didn't see him. I should have because it
was his turn to have me but he phoned last minute on

Saturday morning to say he had an emergency—it turned out that Maxine had decided to chuck Deadbeat Barry out and needed Dad to help in case Deadbeat Barry turned into Deadnasty Barry. I don't know what happened but I know it meant I solved my problem too. Do you remember I was waiting for the right time to talk about the baby with Mum and Jem? Well, it came. I won't bore you with the details but just to let you know everything's OK now.

Oh, and don't worry about school tomorrow—you'll be fine.

PS: Don't forget to meet me back in the form room at break.

Guten Abend

Simone xxx

Simone Wibberley! What do you mean you won't bore me with the details? I have followed the trials and tribulations of your family thus far. It would be cruel of you to exclude me from the main event at this stage. Please let me know what happened—I am all ears and know there won't be an opportunity to speak privately tomorrow.

Ant

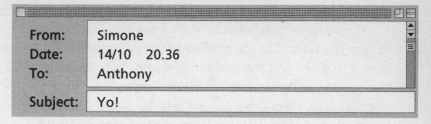

From:	Simone
Date:	14/10 20.36
To:	Anthony
Subject:	Yo!

It's a good job I thought I'd just have one last check of my e-mails before I started on my German homework or I wouldn't have found your reply. Anyway, because I'm not a cruel person, and don't really want to do my German, I will tell you everything. Beware, though, it's another megalonnnnngy!!!!!!

This is what happened. After I put the phone down to Dad, Jem's mum, who was here for that grapefruit visit, asked my mum if 'her father' cancelled often. That got me a bit annoyed. I mean, she could have asked me directly. I was only a breakfast bar away from her. Then Mum replied 'Oh, yes, and the rest,' which annoyed me a bit more again because Dad hasn't missed for ages and *is* doing extra midweek *and* on his Cash and Carry night.

Mrs Cakebread, who'd only been in the house about an hour so it wasn't exactly any of her business, then said, 'Well, that will have to stop when the baby arrives. You can't be doing being messed around like that when you need to establish a routine.' Jem sighed hard and said, 'We know, Mum,' and she said, 'Well, what if you had been going somewhere tonight?' and Jem said, 'We weren't', and she said, 'You might have been', and Jem said, 'But we weren't.' This bit went on for ages so I'll skip it and get to the point.

After loads of this 'what if' stuff from Mrs Cakebread to Jem she turned to me and asked me how old I was now. I told her and she nodded and said, 'Hm! Double the age Jeremy was when his father left us.' So I said, 'My dad didn't leave me, he just left the house,' but she ignored what I thought was a good answer and turned to Jem and said, 'I certainly hope you turn out to be a better father than yours was.' My mum let out this little gasp of air and Jem looked really hurt so I said angrily, 'He already is!' Mrs Cakebread looked puzzled and I could tell she hadn't really understood what I meant. It was obvious she thought his relationship with me didn't count, just as I predicted, so I added, 'And, by the way, I'm not invisible, you know.'

Mum told me not to be rude but I was still angry at *her* for criticizing Dad so I was even ruder and told her she could stop worrying about what will happen when the baby comes because I was already packed and ready to live at Dad's where I knew I was wanted, so whether he turned up for custody time wouldn't be an issue, would it? Whether *she* turned up on time would be the issue then, wouldn't it? We'd see how she coped with having to be at the newsagent's on the dot or you get a deadeye. Ooh, I got into a right strop, Ant. I sounded just like Chloe and flounced off to my bedroom just like she would but with less door-banging because I'm not as experienced.

I sat at my desk for a while trying to read Gillian Cross's letter but my eyes kept going blurry. I know I'm a Y8 and shouldn't be pathetic by crying but sometimes tears just spring up without warning, no matter how old you are. Besides, the letter was laminated so I didn't make the words blotchy, in case you were worried about me ruining original archive material. I didn't realize Jem had come into the room until a huge hanky appeared under my nose. I felt too choked to speak or to tell him off for not knocking when he asked if I was OK, so he just looked at the letter and joked that now it had been laminated we could use it as a place mat, and I sniffed 'no way' even though I knew he was only kidding.

He asked me if I remembered the letters I used to write to him and I said yes and he told me he still had every one of them in a special folder he'd bought from a specialist stationery shop in London. I said I didn't know that and he said, 'Oh, yes, I always take care of precious possessions.' And I said, 'Why my letters, because my spelling was terrible and my handwriting wasn't that great in Year 5 or 6?' but he said without them he would never have met me or my mum and ended up as the happiest man in the world. Actors can say sloppy things without being drunk which is a useful skill to have.

Then he added, 'Thanks for sticking up for me against my mum,' which made me laugh a bit because grown-ups don't need twelve year olds to stick up for them really. Jem explained about how his mum wasn't a bad sort underneath but she had just never recovered from his dad leaving them without a word. She had a broken heart that had never healed. He said having a broken heart that never heals makes you suspicious of everything and you find it hard to trust people. I nodded to show I sort of understood and Jem added,

'She won't be an interfering kind of gran, I promise,' so I just shrugged and said, 'It won't make any difference to me, will it? She's the baby's gran, not mine,' so he asked what I meant and why I had been so upset downstairs.

I wanted to stay angry a bit longer but Jem has a face that doesn't let you so I just told him everything Maxine had said and how I was worried he wouldn't like me any more. It all came out in a hiccuppy mumble but I didn't have to ask if he would treat me the same as the baby because the hug he gave me when I was mid-explanation told me everything I needed to know. It was a real rib-snapper. After he finally let go Jem asked if he could tell Mum and Mrs Cakebread what I'd told him so I said OK, and by the time I felt ready to face everyone *they* were kind of wet round the eyes. Mum gave me another rib-snapper hug and told me I was a big dafty and Mrs Cakebread whipped me straight off into Yeovil for tea and cakes in Denners.

We had this long conversation about what I should call her: Nan or Gran or Grandma or what but in the end we just decided on Angela because that felt the most comfy for both of us. By the time I had finished my third cream doughnut I felt I really knew Angela and quite liked her. Next time she comes to visit, perhaps she could meet up with your gran and go for a pizza or something?

Well, that's it, that's what happened. I feel a bit daft for having thought Mum and Jem would leave me out in the first place. It just shows adults like Maxine don't know everything, like you said in your reply to *Sad of Bartock High*.

Oh no. I've just realized it's past nine o'clock. German's calling—got a double page full of food to label and colour in—better go!

Goodnight, Ant.

Thanks for listening—you're turning into quite a good person for someone who once had a sneery lip!

From: Ant
Date: 14/10   21.45
To: Simone
Subject: Yo!

How many more times! I do not, and never did have, a sneery lip. Honestly!

Apart from that, I'm delighted that you have found stability once more in your family life. It would have been dreadfully bad for the baby to enter a household torn apart through misunderstanding. Have you thought of a name for him/her yet?

Ant

PS: If you read this before tomorrow, I know you're not doing your German again. Shame on you!!

From:	Simone
Date:	14/10 22.00
To:	Ant
Subject:	German

I've finished it, so nah! I think you're right, learning a foreign language isn't so bad once you get the hang of it, especially if it involves colouring in!

Anyway, this is definitely my last e-mail of the night. In fact, I suppose it might be my last e-mail ever to you, because there won't be any need to write to each other, seeing as you're back at school tomorrow.

No, we haven't thought of a name for the baby yet. Everything we think of sounds like a recipe! I'm really, really looking forward to the baby being born though. It's now way bigger than a grapefruit and much more entertaining. Did you know babies can hear sounds and things through the tummy from the outside world? It's true, honest. I can prove it because when I tried telling the baby a few jokes earlier tonight, it moved! It happened every time I told a joke. It seems to like knock-knock jokes best, even the old ones like: Knock, knock, who's there? Isabel. Isabel who? Isabel necessary on a bike? Mum says when it gets near the end of the nine months, you can actually feel the head and toes and bum through the bump, depending on which way the baby's turned. That will be *so* weird!

Anyway,
Goodnight
Don't let the bed bugs bite
See you in the morning
Room 34 at break
OK??
????????

Dear Simone,

I know we could cease e-mailing now like you said in your e-mail last night, but I just wanted to thank you formally for organizing the surprise presentation of the card, cake, and the science revision text book at recess. I did predict you were up to something when you kept repeating instructions to meet in last night's e-mails—a bit of a give-away, if you don't mind my saying. I was particularly relieved to see I had twenty-two signatures on the card this time, none of which appeared to be forgeries. I hope you weren't offended when I let Peter have the vibrant pink fondant appendix decorating the cake. You see, I never eat anything iced pink or red since discovering cochineal is actually made of crushed woodlice from the Americas.

I spent lunchtime in the IT room looking at the All Stars web pages (you never told me about the name—it took me ages to find—I was looking under headings for 'Simone's Website'). I am genuinely impressed with our web pages and I take back what I said about the rotating eyeballs—they are rather innovative and shouldn't cause too much eye-strain. I think we're in with an excellent chance of being selected, despite going well over our page allocation.

One thing I did notice is the Creative Writing Pages seem a little weighted towards poetry. I might consider entering an exclusive extract from *The Golden Spyglass* to redress the balance, if it's not too late.

Ant

I'm glad you liked the cake and card and everything. Big Eurgh if you are right about cochineal!!!!

I've got a titchy favour to ask. Can you meet me in the IT room at lunchtime? I need someone to help finish the web pages because Pete's got a detention for trying to pierce Josh Martin's ear for him with a pair of compasses and Chloe's got a vital appointment staring at Bryce Lambert's lips. They're like velvet, apparently.

As usual I've ended up doing everything, so if you don't have anything on, I'd appreciate your help, unless you need to stare at Bryce Lambert's lips, too?

If you get an early dinner pass from Mr Curbishley, you should still have time to type up your extract and help with the other stuff. Waddya say? See you tomorrow?

Simone

As I am not in the habit of staring at people's lips I think
you can rest assured I'll be in the IT room lunchtime.
  Your reliable colleague,

  Ant

Thanks, Anthony—you're a mate! (no offence!)

  Simone

Welcome to the ALL STARS Web Pages

The ALL STARS are:
(in alphabetical order)

Peter Bacon *Anthony Bent*
Chloe Shepherd *Simone Wibberley*

We are all in Mr Curbishley's class, 8DC

We hope you enjoy this site.
We think it has something for everyone.

Read about children's writer Gillian Cross's visit to Bartock High during Book Week

Read poetry and prose by Year 8s

Do you have a problem? Check out our problem page and get not one but four points of view from each of the All Stars

Find out how well we're doing in sports this season on our league tables and read an interview with ace striker Oliver Woodman

Choose a link

- Sports news
- Book news
- Problem Page
- Creative Writing
- Special Features:
  Ten weapons you need by your bed at all times in case of attack
- How 2 tell if your gal or guy is right 4U—one All Star's advice

 Next ▸▸

◄◄ Back to homepage

Bartock High School Year Eight Sports News

Netball	Football (Boys)	Basketball	Football (Girls)
Results: Lost: 1 Won: 1 Drawn: 0	Results: Lost: 1 Won: 3 Drawn: 1	Results: Lost: 1 Won: 0 Drawn: 0	Results: Lost: 0 Won: 3 Drawn: 0
The Year 8 team has only played two matches so far. They lost to in-form Ansford 10–4 but won at home to Stocklinch 7–2 Captain Josephine Lyons declined to be interviewed.	The Year 8 team is looking as strong as ever, despite the absence of striker Anthony Bent whose appendix exploded during drama this term. The season began with a resounding 4–0 victory over St Paul's. Two Y8 players, Oliver Woodman and Daniel O'Connell, have been selected for Yeovil Town's youth programme.	The High Hoops, as they have named their team, did not get off to a very good start when they played The Chard Sharks. They would not reveal the exact results but it was in high figures to nil. Their captain, Bryce Lambert said: 'OK, we were stuffed but they were much taller than us.'	The girls' team is not all Year Eights—it's a mix of Y7 to Y9s. They put their flying start down to wondergirl Melanie McCleod. Melanie's only a Y7 but has already scored 6 goals in three matches. Captain Evelyn Maresma says; 'Mel's brilliant. She's fast and nippy and scares the opposition to death. Once she has the ball, she won't let go.'* *This does not surprise me. I used to watch Mel when she played on the team at Woodhill Primary School. Some boys thought it would be easy to tackle a girl but how wrong they were!! Ed*

 Next page for more sports news ►►

◀◀ **Back**

An Interview with football captain Oliver Woodman
by Chloe Shepherd

I interviewed drop-dead gorgeous football captain Oliver 'Eye Candy' Woodman at the beginning of the season. Tall, dark, and well tasty, I asked him what it was like to play football for the school. He replied in a well dishy voice, 'OK.' Looking deep into his awesome blue eyes, I asked him how long he had played the game. The answer was, since he was six. Do you dream of playing for England? I questioned further. 'No,' he replied, 'I'm Welsh. I want to follow in the footsteps of Ryan Giggs and score for Wales.' Well, I think all the popular girls will agree with me that we want to follow in your footsteps and score with you, Oliver!!!!!!

A photograph of Oliver Woodman scoring one of his 19 goals against some other team last season. Doesn't he look well lush, even covered in mud?

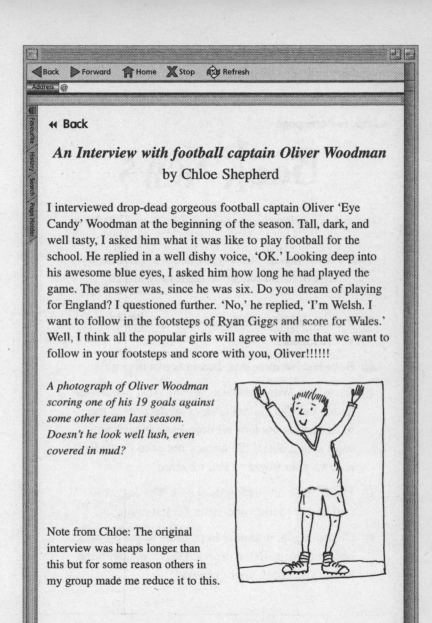

Note from Chloe: The original interview was heaps longer than this but for some reason others in my group made me reduce it to this.

◀◀ back to homepage

Book News

The following pages were compiled by Simone Wibberley

I have been helping Mrs Jagger in the library this term.
I have found out some interesting things:

- Year Sevens borrow the most books out of the whole school.

- Boys borrow more non-fiction books than girls.

- Jacqueline Wilson's books are the most popular in fiction but *The Guinness Book of Records* is the most popular book of all time, even though you can't take it out of the library, not even if you stuff it down your trousers, Peter Bacon!

- Pupils leave disgusting things for Mrs Jagger to find on her shelves and stuck behind radiators.

- Chewing gum is almost impossible to get off desks once it hardens in the cracks. Please, please, think before you chuck your chewwy!!

◀◀ back to previous page more on book week ▶▶

Book Week
October 15th-19th

During <u>Book Week</u> Mrs Jagger organized a sale of books in the library. She doesn't know how much money was raised yet but she feels it was a success. In assemblies, teachers read from their favourite children's books. Everyone laughed when Mr Curbishley read his favourite, *Hairy Maclarey from Donaldson's Dairy* by Lynley Dodds. The *peak of the week* for me was on Thursday when the author <u>Gillian Cross</u> visited our school. I was really excited about meeting her because I have never met a real writer before. I was surprised to find she looked like a normal person. I found it very interesting listening to how she writes and where she gets her ideas from. I was a bit fed up because other people in my group asked her the questions I wanted to ask so I never got to speak to her directly but fortunately I had written to her before her visit and found out all I needed to know. The other annoying part was 8DC were on first dinners so we couldn't queue up for an autograph like 8AW could or we'd get done by the supervisors.

If anyone wants to read my special letter from Gillian Cross, Mrs Jagger has photocopied it and put it on the notice board next to the picture of Count Dracula. The original has been laminated and is at my house (letter, not Dracula). I am in the middle of one of Gillian's books, *Tightrope*, and it is very good so far, full of excitement and tension, but if you want to borrow it after me you might have to wait a bit because I am busy with homework and things at the moment and won't be returning it for a couple of weeks.

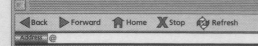

Problem Page

Your four agony buds are:

Peter Bacon

Qualifications: Peter is a good listener and comes from a large family so he is an expert on anything to do with sharing and coping with being bullied by an older, much uglier brother.

Chloe Shepherd

Qualifications: Chloe has been reading *J17* since she was in Y7 and shaving her legs since she was in Y6 and feels she knows all there is to know on relationships and skincare.

Anthony Bent

Qualifications: Anthony is an intellectual and free-thinker. He specializes in homework worries or strategies for improving lateral thinking. He has a high IQ but won't reveal how high in case it causes friction.

Simone Wibberley

Qualifications: Simone is also a good listener with experience on health problems such as asthma and family problems such as parents who are divorced and use too much sarcasm during visits in front of their children.

◀◀ previous page   next page ▶▶

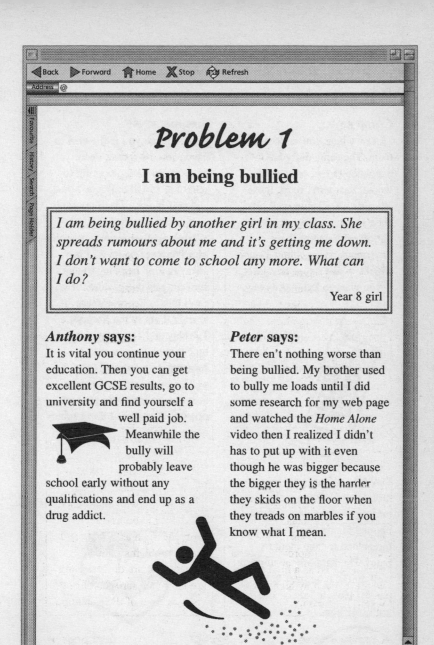

Problem 1

I am being bullied

I am being bullied by another girl in my class. She spreads rumours about me and it's getting me down. I don't want to come to school any more. What can I do?

Year 8 girl

Anthony says:

It is vital you continue your education. Then you can get excellent GCSE results, go to university and find yourself a well paid job. Meanwhile the bully will probably leave school early without any qualifications and end up as a drug addict.

Peter says:

There en't nothing worse than being bullied. My brother used to bully me loads until I did some research for my web page and watched the *Home Alone* video then I realized I didn't has to put up with it even though he was bigger because the bigger they is the harder they skids on the floor when they treads on marbles if you know what I mean.

103

Chloe says:

I know where you're coming from. The same thing has happened to me, only much worse. Last term, right, these Y9 girls were being well bit-chee about me just because I got off with one of their boyfriends on the Alton Towers trip. He wasn't even that tasty, if you want to know. Anyway,

they kept phoning me on my mobile and leaving sicko messages, right, so my mum phoned their parents and threatened to take them to court. The harassment stopped well quick. It helps if your parents have influence and dine with solicitors.

Simone says:

It must make you feel awful to have rumours spread about you but you must keep coming to school or it will only get worse and you'll never catch up with your lessons on top of everything else. Have you seen Mrs Warrener about it? I have always found her easy to talk to and she gets things done. If you can't talk to her or another teacher, I am in the library on Tuesday and Thursday lunchtimes if you want someone to come with you. I will be in the reference section next week displaying reviews of <u>Book Week</u> but I don't mind being disturbed.

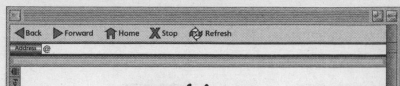

Problem 2

Spot of bother

My face and back are covered in spots. I have tried creams but nothing seems to work. I hate going out because I am so embarrassed. Any suggestions?

Tamla Kershaw 8DC

Anthony says:

I know from the number of column inches I read on skin 'problems' in magazines during my recent stay in hospital such things are meant to be taken seriously but I think a sense of perspective is needed here. Have you seen the film *Elephant Man*, about the distressing life of Mr Joseph Merrick of Victorian England? He had such hideous deformities it looked as if he had cauliflowers growing out of his face. Now there was a man with something to complain about. You can read all about him on any number of websites. His remains are to be found in the Royal London Hospital.

Chloe says:

You must just want to die!!!!!!!!!!!!!! I know I would if I had anything less than perfect skin. I would never dare be seen outside. It must be a relief for you not to have a boyfriend because you'd be wondering whether he'll dump you when you have a bad spot day. I have heard that Zit-Zap is effective but it is rather expensive so you probably won't be able to buy any.

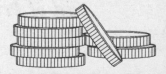

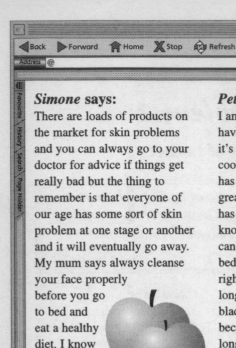

Simone says:

There are loads of products on the market for skin problems and you can always go to your doctor for advice if things get really bad but the thing to remember is that everyone of our age has some sort of skin problem at one stage or another and it will eventually go away. My mum says always cleanse your face properly before you go to bed and eat a healthy diet. I know you already do both those things so there's nothing else you can do, Tamla. By the way, even though I don't think looks or clothes are important, I think you are one of the prettiest girls in our year, not that you ever believe me.

Peter says:

I am really jealous because I haven't got any spots yet and it's not fair because they look cool. My brother and his friends has tons of spots and they has great times with theirs. They has competitions. Like, did you know the yellow stuff inside can shoot across your entire bedroom if you pop it just right? Also, my brother keeps a long wormy bit from a squizzed blackhead in his pencil tin because he is so proud of how long it is (5.3cm). I tried to see if it would make the *Guinness Book of Records* but got caught trying to take the book out. I was going to give it back but I'm a slow reader, not that nobody believed me. Your face always looks all right to me, Tam. I'd snog it without puking any day.

End of Problem Page

◄◄ Back to homepage   **creative writing ►►**

The **ALL STARS** Creative Writing Page

The Sea

In the deepest, darkest depths of the sea,
The dolphins swim while the fishes flee,
The sharks, they prowl, like hunting cats,
Looking for prey like cats eating rats.
The seals swim and sniff the air
The manatee laughs, tickling the air
The blue whale,
Graceful, peaceful, rarest giant
Although the ocean is wondrous as can be,
Why do we want to destroy the sea?

Joshua Martin 8AW

Cool poem, Josh! Ed.

The **ALL STARS** would like to thank Mr Pikelet of the English Department for letting us use his Creative Writing Club's poems. (The Club meets in the library every Wednesday lunchtime between 12.30 and 1.10pm. Bring a pen)

◀◀ **Back to homepage**　　　◉◉　　**more creative writing** ▶▶

❤ First Kiss ❤

I was in France when it happened. My parents had sent me to a Kids Club there for the summer holidays. To get a feel for the continent, they said. To get out of their way more like. I was gutted.

The first two days were exactly as I expected—no en suite bathroom, no satellite TV, no decent food—it was the pits. Until William arrived. William was well gorgeous. He was thirteen, tall and confident with a smile that could kill. I made sure I sat next to him every meal time and during French tutorials, despite competition from older girls with no idea how to apply make-up. I soon found out his likes and dislikes and spent nearly all my allowance on a replica Manchester United shirt for him. He was overwhelmed, I knew, but very shy. I determined I had to feel his lips on mine, just once, before I left for home. The night before the end of my stay we had a disco. I played it really cool all night until the end when I went up to him and asked him for a dance.

He said yes. I flung my arms around him and planted a whopper on his lips. He tasted of Polos and love. William was so overcome with emotion, he had to leave and I didn't see him again. Bad Make-Up girl said it was because he was avoiding me but I knew the truth. William just couldn't stand the thought of never seeing me again, so he put on a brave face. Though I have dated many boys since, I will never forget William, or the summer of my first kiss when I was nearly twelve years old.

Chloe Madelaine Shepherd

Pass the sick bag—Ed

108

An exclusive extract from *The Golden Spyglass*

The first of a planned trilogy by Anthony B. Bent

Reproduced only on the understanding that no part of this story may be photocopied or used in any way without the author's permission which he does not grant.

Chapter One
The Mysterious Discovery

The squat, red-faced, stern but occasionally jovial housekeeper of St Wilfreda's Orphanage was not in the best of moods that morning when she went to fetch in the milk. For a start, menial milk-fetching was clearly not a job for her but the flighty maid, Connie Warren, was, as usual, nowhere to be seen.

Puffing and panting as she hauled back first one then another of the heavy bolts which kept the orphans of St Wilfreda's in and the intruders of Wolvercote near Oxford out, Mrs Heckmondwyke muttered to herself bitterly.

On the doorstep she stared in disgust. Next to the dozens of bottles of skimmed and semi-skimmed but hardly any full-fat milk, was a tiny moses basket and what's more, it was moving. Mrs Heckmondwyke stepped closer and shook her grey, curly, short, neat hair. Not another baby! she thought to herself. But this one was different. There was a parchment note attached to its blanket. The note said, in a beautiful, well-crafted obviously educated hand: 'Whomsoever should take care of this child will one day be rewarded with riches a-plenty.'

How strange, thought Mrs Heckmondwyke, closing the door behind her. She did not notice the figure of a mere slip of a lass in grimy, dirty rags disappearing round the corner of the wide, sweeping street. And thus the mysterious story beginneth . . .

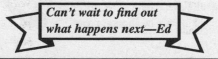

Can't wait to find out what happens next—Ed

◀◀ **back to creative writing and arts page**　**on to next page** ▶▶

109

More poems from Mr Pikelet's Creative Writing Club

Nothing

Nothing isn't nothing
It is something
So if you have nothing
You do have something
You have NOTHING

Charelle Griffith 8CH

> **I have nothing more to say, Charelle—nothing more—get it?—Ed**

Brothers

B rothers, brothers
R otten and disgusting
O ut of his bedroom comes loud music
T here he is having a temper
H orrible habits
E ating and dropping crumbs everywhere
R evolting sounds come from out of his belly
S melly like a sock, that's brothers for you.

Nazia Khan 8CH

> **Peter Bacon totally agrees with you on this one, Naz!!!—Ed**

1976 is the Year

1976 is the year
The memory's still with us clear
The fight was about education
The fight was about civilization
The outcome was supposed to be positive
But unfortunately it became negative

Out of all this outcome there was one voice
Which represented the nation
One voice for equal opportunity and freedom
Instead of hearing this voice a riot broke out
Freedom seekers and opportunities, lost lives

This all happened in Soweto in 1976

Fazia Farooq

> **I'm glad I don't live there, Fazia—Ed**

An ALL STARS Special Feature
Ten Things You Need By Your Bed
At All Times In Case Of Attack

WRITTEN AND DRAWN BY Peter Bacon

Introduction.

Your bedroom is a sacred place. It is where you go to get peace and quiet
from your family after a hard day's slog in prison (aka school). But what
happens when that peace is shattered by intruders? I'm thinking not just
of burglars and ghosts, but big hairy smelly brothers who think they can
barge on to your side any time and touch your stuff and mess with your
things. This is my tips for you.

I have used only things you can get locally from toy shops or art rooms
or your mum's tool shed. If your mum or dad or foster carer is in the
army or police, you can get miles better stuff but mine isn't, worst luck,
so I had to use my brains to think up stuff.

Here goes:

1. *Marbles*

These is your obvious choice, esp. if you has wooden
flooring—put them around your bedroom floor and see
that big brother skid!!!!!! Hee-haw!!

2. *Mouse traps*

Put these on top of your desk or at the bottom of your
wardrobe so when the intruder is fumbling in the dark
for your stuff they will get a nasty nip and their
screams will wake you up then you can whack them
on the head with:

111

3. a *plastic baseball bat* which has got to hurt, guys.

4. For under your pillow—a *Super Snapper water pistol* from all good supermarkets. Keep it loaded at all times but don't forget to plug the stopper in real good or the water dribbles out all over your pillow and your brother teases you about crying like a baby even when you weren't never.

5. *Plastic dog-do and plastic vomit*

This is great for spooking people because if you puts it next to your ham and Cheerios sandwich you have made yourself for supper, then you need to go to the toilet and your brother or dad comes in, they don't nick the sandwich off of you so much.

6. *Treacle or honey on the window sill*

This works dead well for stopping burglars in their tracks if they is climbing through your window except remember to clean it when your mum or dad comes in to do the windows or look for cups and plates and mucky underpants because they get mad when they put their hands in treacle and won't listen to reason and say you is taking this whole SAS thing too far when they don't know nothing. Treacle is also Highly Recommended in summer for trapping noisy bluebottles and hornets and moths but it does look a bit nasty when they lies there not quite dead, kicking their little legs about.

7. *Posters of ladies with not many clothes on*

This will distract the burglar or your brother and put them in a trance so you can call the police. I know for certain it works for my brother. It might not work for a lady burglar, I suppose.

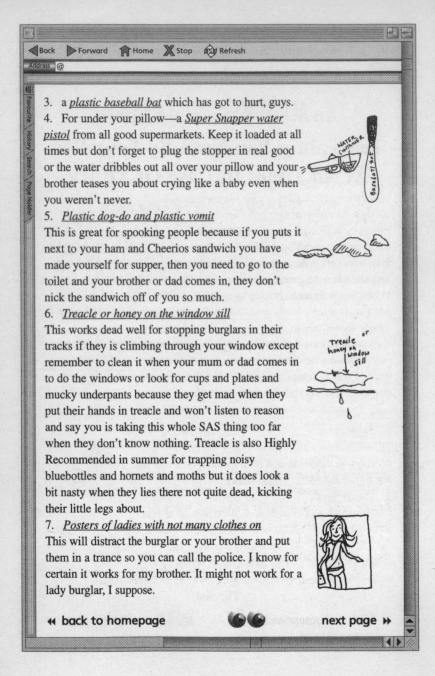

8. *Stickle bricks on the carpet*

These really hurt bare feet when the burglar or your brother is trying to sneak across and strangle you in the dark. Lego is good, too, or Playmobile or staples.

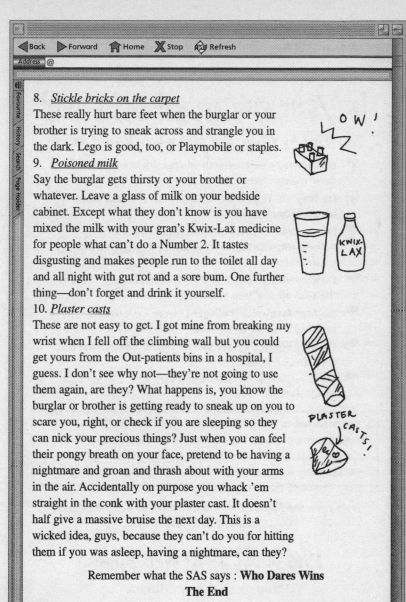

9. *Poisoned milk*

Say the burglar gets thirsty or your brother or whatever. Leave a glass of milk on your bedside cabinet. Except what they don't know is you have mixed the milk with your gran's Kwix-Lax medicine for people what can't do a Number 2. It tastes disgusting and makes people run to the toilet all day and all night with gut rot and a sore bum. One further thing—don't forget and drink it yourself.

10. *Plaster casts*

These are not easy to get. I got mine from breaking my wrist when I fell off the climbing wall but you could get yours from the Out-patients bins in a hospital, I guess. I don't see why not—they're not going to use them again, are they? What happens is, you know the burglar or brother is getting ready to sneak up on you to scare you, right, or check if you are sleeping so they can nick your precious things? Just when you can feel their pongy breath on your face, pretend to be having a nightmare and groan and thrash about with your arms in the air. Accidentally on purpose you whack 'em straight in the conk with your plaster cast. It doesn't half give a massive bruise the next day. This is a wicked idea, guys, because they can't do you for hitting them if you was asleep, having a nightmare, can they?

Remember what the SAS says : **Who Dares Wins**
The End

Is Your guy or gal right 4U?

Top Tips by Chlo, the girl who should know

❓ Do they take care over their appearance 4U and not wear cheap clothes?

❓ **Do they tell U how fab U look even if U ask them like, a zillion tymz?**

❓ Do they put U B 4 everything Lse such az homework, visiting sick rellies, c-ing their other mates?

❓ **Do they always pay 4 U 2 go 2 sit in the best seats at the cinema and buy you Haagen Das?**

❓ Do they forgive U if U 4get U were suppost 2B meeting them and they end up waiting in the rain?

❓ **Do they agree 2 ignore people U don't like, even if they do like them?**

❓ Do they get well jealous when they C U flirting with someone?

If you answered no to any of these, you should seriously think about dumping your gal or guy. There's nothing 2 it—just text them with the simple message U R Dumpt or ignore them next time you see them. Laughing with your best mate as they approach can b fun 2.

Note from the Editor: Dump unto others as you would have dumped unto you!!!

End of ALL STARS Web Pages

Hope you enjoyed them.

◀◀ **back to previous page**

From: Anthony
Date: 04/02   16.32
To: Simone
Subject: Our turn on the website

Dear Simone,

Gosh! It seems like yonks since I e-mailed you. October, in fact. Funny how quickly we returned to our previous habits once I settled back in at Bartock High.

Anyway, you were away today and I wondered whether you had realized it was the first day for the All Stars web pages to go live on the school site? You'll be relieved to know they scroll perfectly and are far better to navigate than any other group's efforts, even Oliver's, despite our setbacks. I feel we should have had a much higher grade than the feeble Level 5/6 Miss Brighton awarded us.

Anyway, that's all I have to say, really.

Sincerely

Anthony (I have returned to my full name now, in case you didn't know).

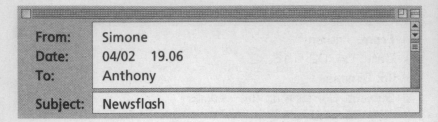

Dear Anthony,

Thanks for the e-mail. Yes, it is yonks since we've e-mailed, and, yes, I did remember about our web pages but I was involved in something much more important. Remember my mum was pregnant and I told you all about it? Well . . . Wait for it . . . I have a new baby sister! Mum went into labour just as I was about to leave for the bus this morning. I could still have come to school but Jem seemed to forget every single thing he'd learned at Parentcraft classes. He couldn't concentrate on anything apart from holding on to Mum when she had a contraction. I stuck the list of things to do under his nose but, like me with algebra and German verbs, he just couldn't take it in so I called Dad and he came immediately.

I suppose you might think it was a weird thing for an ex-husband to be taking his ex-wife to hospital with his ex-wife's partner and a daughter who belonged to them all but it seemed like a good idea at the time. I guess it would have been more tense if Alexis had come but she's having a closing down sale for *Stars in your Size* (don't ask!) so everything's more of a nightmare than ever and she was in no state to assist.

It was nice having Dad with me, especially when they rushed Mum and Jem straight into the delivery room. I heard one of the midwives say to a nurse, 'She's fully dilated,' as she passed, which I know from my research means 'on your marks'. Dad and I just looked at each other. I thought he'd want to get straight back to the shop but instead he bought me a hot chocolate from a machine and told me all about what happened when I was being born. He doesn't usually talk about things like that, so I was really interested. Mum was in labour with me for twenty-two hours, apparently. I was the wrong way round and everything and Dad got into an argument with one of the doctors because they wanted to use these forceps things and Dad said he didn't want a baby with a head shaped like something from *Star Trek*. In the end I turned round by myself and came out in the perfect form you see before you today (though a lot smaller, obviously).

As we were on the subject, I asked Dad if he was going to have a baby with Alexis but he shook his head and said not for all the tea in China. I said I thought it was a good decision.

About four hot chocolates later, Jem stuck his head round the door and beamed, 'It's a girl.' Dad said, 'What about Cathy? How is she?' and Jem said 'Fine. Absolutely fine.' He had tears in his eyes. Dad nodded and there were tears in *his* eyes that made me feel like crying, too, though I'm not sure why. He shook Jem's hand then suddenly remembered the drinks man was coming and he was totally out of Irn Bru so he left.

A few minutes later I was allowed in. I kissed Mum first, who looked a bit sweaty but otherwise normal, then hugged Jem, then guess what? They said I could hold my baby sister! She's called Isabel Grace and weighs seven pounds and eleven ounces but doesn't feel it. I don't usually go in for baby stuff much but it is different when you are related and Izzie's gorgeous—all tiny and so sweet with a mass of dark hair. I talked to her and promised her I would protect her forever, then she fell asleep and the nurse put her in this see-through cot thing. Holding her is just the best, so there was no chance of me coming back to school, even though I could have made it for period four.

It is such a relief being able to call Isabel Isabel instead of 'it' or 'the baby' all the time. If her name rings a bell, it's because we chose it from those knock-knock jokes I used to tell her when she was inside Mum's tum. (Rings a bell—get it?)

Anyway, I just thought you'd like to know!

Come and see Izzie at the weekend if you want. Tamla and Mel will probably be there, and Chloe, seeing as she's been calling round a lot recently since she fell out with Josephine Lyons (again) and needs someone to moan to about her tragic love life. Bring Oliver, if you like. That should distract her!

Bis bald

Simone Anna Wibberley—Isabel Grace's big sister.

Dear Simone,

Congratulations on becoming a sibling. Mother has contacted Interflora on behalf of us all, so expect something in cellophane soon. Meanwhile, I chose this card for you—sorry if it is a bit 'pink' for your liking but, as with the 'Get Well' cards back in September, your father's stock is somewhat lacking in choice (no offence, as you might say!) Your father did send his regards when I told him for whom the purchase was being made and knocked fifty p. off my Orienteering Monthly which was generous of him. I'll e-mail Oliver and see if he'd like to visit. Do we need to wear protective clothing?

Anthony

Why not visit the real, live All Stars website at
www.oup.com/uk/simone

Look at what you'll find:

- A Sports page – uncut and uncensored exclusive interview with Oliver Woodman

- A Problem page – with answers to all those tricky questions from Bartock High pupils

- A Book Recommendations page – with all those other books you should be reading

- A Creative Writing page – your chance to send us your poems

- An "About" page – read about the author and illustrator of Simone books

- An Interview with Gillian Cross page – find out the answers to all of the All Stars questions to Gillian

- A Competition page – your chance to WIN £100 of OUP Children's books, plus a signed copy of this book!

And keep an eye out for those rolling eyeballs!!!
(eye out – get it? eyes?)

Other books by Helena Pielichaty

Simone's Letters

ISBN 0 19 275287 1

*Dear Mr Cakebread . . . For starters my name is Simone, not Simon . . .
Mum says you sound just like my dad. My dad, Dennis, lives in
Bartock with his girlfriend, Alexis . . . My mum says lots of rude
things about her because Alexis was one of the reasons my parents got
divorced (I was the other) . . .*

When ten-year-old Simone starts writing letters to Jem Cakebread,
the leading man of a touring theatre company, she begins a
friendship that will change her life . . . and the lives of all around her:
her mum, her best friend Chloe, her new friend Melanie—and not
forgetting Jem himself!

This collection of funny and often touching letters charts Simone's
final year at Primary School; from a school visit to *Rumpelstiltskin's
Revenge* to her final leaving Assembly; through the ups and downs
of her friendships—and those of her mum and dad.

'Wickedly perceptive about school life, the 10-year-old female psyche
and parental separation, this is a laugh-out-loud, feel-good book written
with vivacious wit.'
> *The Times Educational Supplement*

'This is a sparkling story . . . The treatment of the aftermath of divorce, the
friendship of schoolgirls, everyday school life . . . is accurate, touching and
funny.'
> *School Librarian Journal*

'It's a skilful and original unwinding of primary school life and its concerns
as well as the anxieties of family life.'
> *The Independent*

Simone's Diary

ISBN 0 19 275288 X

Dear Mr Cohen . . . Hi, it's me, Simone Anna Wibberley. Do you remember me from when you were a student on teaching practice with Miss Cassidy's class? . . . I am applying to be in your experiment . . . I will answer everything as fully as I can . . . I am quite good at this sort of thing because I used to fill in a lot of questionnaires in magazines with my dad's ex-girlfriend, Alexis . . .

Simone has left Woodhill Primary School behind her and is starting life at her new secondary school. It's a little bit scary and there are lots of new things to get used to, so when she's asked to take part in an experiment by writing a diary and filling in questionnaires about her new experiences at Bartock High School, it's the perfect opportunity for Simone to write down all her thoughts and ideas in her own inimitable style.

'I warmed to Simone and her realistic approach to life—she's Adrian Mole without the angst.'
    School Librarian